This book is a work of fiction. Names, characters, places and incidents are wholly fictional or are used fictionally. Any resemblance to persons living or dead is entirely coincidental.

Cover art by Keron Grant

Color by Silver Phoenix Entertainment

Edited by Gail Edmonds

First run proudly printed in the U.S.A by Silver Phoenix Entertainment Inc.

Acknowledgements

Special thanks to Keron Grant, Gail Edmonds, William Hiyashi and Blue 1647 for contributing their time, and wisdom.

Contents

MERMAID MARINES

4

Chapter 1

A Dream Have I

CARCINE didn't know what had taken hold of him. Standing at the center of what was left of Rayla's storm, shock consumed him. He couldn't even shake his head in disgust, looking over the broken glass in his once pristine nightclub, Rhiannon. Shangos, Neo Astronauts, Planet Hope…he would rather think it was all a dream. Even his Earthly love, Luba, was gone. He shoved a pile of shaven glass to the side with his foot, crouched down, and pulled out a red feather. It was all that remained of Rayla Redfeather—in this world at least.

"So what are you going to do?" a woman's voice cooed. Eleven Brown emerged from the shadows. Arms folded and clad in her trademark black, she walked deliberately with a sway that Carcine liked. Dark brown eyes and mossy black hair fluffed.back in a ponytail, she paused near the heap of twisted, broken lights.

"How'd you get in here?"

"I'm Eleven, Eleven Brown."

A smile crept across Carcine's face. He'd heard the stories. "Well this must be my lucky day."

"You have no idea," she said, wrinkling her nose.

"Didn't know you were real," he said. "You here to clean up?"

"But of course."

"And I guess you're taking me to the water."

"How'd you guess?"

***

Carcine liked this lake of five. It wasn't purple like Planet Hope, but it had a cold practicality to its liquid touch that he'd grown to like. The water met the sandy shore's edge, and the soft waves stopped as he and Eleven ebbed closer.

"How does this work exactly?" he asked.

A gust of wind blew and Eleven stared in its direction.

"We go below and you'll be king of the sea."

"Will I grow fins?" he asked.

Eleven smiled tightly. "Everyone asks that," she added. Carcine surveyed the lake's surface then scanned the building tops that brushed against the horizon, soaking it all in as if he'd never see it again. "You'll soon discover that the terrestrial life is overrated," Eleven said firmly. Carcine tried not to think of Rayla, his distant love far beyond the stratosphere. He didn't want his treasured last moments on this land to be thoughts of her. She made her choice. Eleven pulled her new friend out of wonderment. She turned her hypnotizing gaze from Carcine to the lake of five and dove in, her legs morphing into the ivygreen Mermaid tail he'd read about. So she is real, he thought, smiling to himself. Carcine dove in behind her. His legs morphing into a silver tail didn't frighten him the way he'd anticipated. In fact, he rather liked it. Breathing water, he discovered, was intoxicating.

"What do they call this place again?" he asked, navigating below the water's lighter edge beside Eleven. A school of giant bass glided by.

"We call it Ku," she said. "You do remember the land of Ku?" she asked.

"Oh, yeah," he said, remembering the lush East African life so many centuries ago. He liked that life. He adored that impossible Princess, the one he almost wed. Another Rayla-in-waiting hang glider he'd decided to shut from his waking days. "How'd it get under here?" he asked.
"Long story," she said, dipping below a hearty reef.

"But first you must meet the mother fish," she said.

"I thought that was you," he interjected.

"No, I'm just an enlightened distraction," she cooed.

Carcine liked distractions. He was amusing himself with thoughts of his new life when he noticed it. The underwater city glistened like a million fireflies. At the heart stood an enormous Sphinx,-glowing a hue of green so beautiful he was nearly spellbound. He was drawn to it. She, the woman who called this Sphinx home, was obviously everywhere. Moulan Shakur, the mystic with no past, was seated deep within the Sphinx chamber and was watching. From that epic distance, Carcine couldn't see her, but he felt her response sing in his mind. He'd know that voice anywhere. "Yes, I am, darling, everywhere. And don't you forget it."

Chapter 2

Alright Be Gonna We

SOME people like the hope of the rising sun, but I'm attracted to the glowing night moon. Yes, Obama City's vibrant allure is the hope of my people's galactic toils, but it's the silent noise of nature I find myself gravitating to when I need a bit of me. I am Rayla Illmatic. I like saying this under the moonlight, as I just did. I relish in the idea that my voice carries, that sound goes beyond the rainbows, and that somewhere beyond this realm my self-assertion needs to be heard. It's a cozy thought I think to justify saying it to myself and then aloud as I stand on the edge of the Enchanted Forest, leaning against this towering maple tree as I breath in simpler moments.

My life had changed. Once all of The Missing were recovered, people emerged from Sebastian's Cave and the work of re-erecting our jewel in the sky continued. A new government was established, new elected officials, new schools, and new work to be done. I worked as an organizer, a city planner who helped craft the structure of our new land. The work was fairly smooth, due to the people's enthusiasm. Everyone agreed to whatever worked best, so we moved pretty swiftly. Eartha Mandela, former Neo Astronaut and mother of Delta Blue was elected president; Lagos, former Neo Astronaut was vice president; my father Kent was chief philosopher at our reinstated school of Demeter.

Everyone wanted me to run for office, but I refused. They mounted a write-in campaign anyway, and I was reluctantly elected into the council. I resigned, but Eartha wanted to appease the people and believed that I must serve. She created a title of sorts for me. I would be Statesperson at Large, consulting on galactic matters. They wanted me to reinstitute the space program. I recommended Delta instead, but Delta, much like me, was trying to shirk these new organizational duties, too. I was a war strategist, and he was a warrior. Where did we fit in peace?

When the towers in Obama City were erected, I was given a sprawling dwelling in the sky, atop the new Illmatic Center, a tribute edifice to my work, my father's work, and an honor to the Neo Astronauts. They erected statues. A statue of me, a chiseled marble one that echoed ancient times, sat at the center of the city. The city folk, in their "back to life" jubilee enthusiasm, were raining honors, and a Rayla Day was even in the works. It was nice, I suppose, but this newfound popularity in peaceful times was a bit uncomfortable. Obama City's celebratory galas outnumbered the elites of Shogun City's at this point.

Someone came up with the grand idea to honor each day of celebration by sporting a gigantic hat of colors. From feather plumes to galactic cowboy, these hats were a rainbow of clustered flowers from my dwelling in the sky. They called this day, the Day of Return, in commemoration of the final Neo Astronauts' homecoming. It was a glamorama of lighted spectacles, and I was the must-attend guest for all of it. But I needed to be alone. Another festival was not what I needed, so I escaped to the Enchanted Forest. I sat against the maple's trunk and looked across the horizon of yellow. Once upon a time, a woman lived in a virtual home. Memories.I suppose everyone was happy. But I didn't share their glee, and the guilt of it all had me a bit glum.

It seemed that the reconstruction of our society was the answer to everyone's question. No one referenced our time travel. There were talks about reconnecting with Earth, but after that fiasco in Chicagotropolis and the wanton discovery that we Planet Hopers were a myth, it was determined that Earth's governments were too hostile; and for the sake of self-preservation, it was best that we keep to ourselves. I disagreed, but with this new government emerging and the horrific experiences of the Neo Astronauts as not so distant history, all agreed that the matter would be tabled, for now. No one seemed to care much that Shogun City was still the Shogun City of old, largely closed to the masses with a full army. The two cities were hospitable, friendlier than the past, but this mantra of live and let live prevailed and Shogun City continued its policies. The underground mazes were open, but in these times who needed them.

No one, it seemed, wanted to talk much about Moulan either. Moulan, the architect of the Neo Astronaut program, vanished in our rescue operation in Chicagotropolis—the rescue operation that recovered the astronauts, including my own father. The strings from Earth to Obama City were blocked on the Shogun City end, and it was assumed that Moulan had imploded. But in those final moments when the Shangos, the Neo Astronauts, the Outkast, Delta, Carcine, and I were in battle, Moulan revealed that she was my mother – a revelation that shocked no one but me. No one wanted to talk about it.

My father, whom I loved, wanted to skirt past those missing, messy years. He talked a bit about his experiences on Earth, but he devoted most of his moments with me to rejoicing in the peace of the times. He talked about missing Planet Hope's fresh air and vibrant crystals. He waxed poetically about our planet's values; and on occasion, he joked about his athletic feats. However, he had little to no interest in discussing the past and virtually no desire to explain Moulan.

"Moulan and I had a bond," he said. "You are a result of that bond," he added. "But she is no one to me now, and she should be no one to you ever."

Sui Lee's response wasn't much different. She and my father

were committed life partners. They shared a nice crystal dome home in Obama City's historic district. The two of us were drinking tea in her crystal garden when I asked about Moulan. "Remember the values of the sisterhood, Rayla. That Moulan experience was a brief moment. Don't let it define you."
I didn't press it.

But here in the Enchanted Forest, I could almost see where the virtual home used to be. I heard a rustling in the vines two paces behind me. "It's just me, Rayla," Delta said, pushing a hanging vine from his path. "How'd you know I was out here?" I asked. "Lucky guess," he said. "Not one for the star life, I see," he said. Delta at one point in life was used to constant adulation. But even this, in the midst of our return was a bit much.

After our return, Delta and I spent much of our time together. We acknowledged our soul-mate connection and honored the bond of sharing old and new lives across time. He wasn't as sarcastic as he used to be. I didn't block his mind-reading abilities, and we silently agreed to grow together. We knew one another and found comfort in our inexplicable bond when the New Planet Hope overwhelmed us.

"I want to see her," I said. "I want to see Moulan, to talk to her," I added. But I wasn't looking at Delta. I kept my eyes toward the Field of the Yellow Lady. "I need to know her story."

"You have her book," he said sheepishly.

"I want to hear it from her," I retorted.

"Well, that's as close as you're gonna get, Rayla," he said softly, too softly for the depth of his voice.

"My father won't tell me anything," I said. He crouched down beside me, leaning against the great Maple, and closed his eyes.

"We should go back to the festival," he said. "Everyone's asking about you." But before Delta could finish his sentence, I was dashing across the thick field of Yellow. I ran because I needed the rush of air in

my lungs. I ran because I needed to see it. I needed to see if the virtual world still stood. I didn't stop to see if Delta was behind me. I could feel him on my heels. He yearned to know, too. But halfway through the field I stopped running. It wasn't the shortness of breath that made me fall to the ground, although I was tired. I stopped because there was no virtual world on the otherside. I couldn't bear to see more of the thorny yellow in its absence. I cried, my face planted in the moist blue soil. Delta stroked my back, eased me up, and together we walked back. By the time we cut through the Forest and back into the city the festival was over.

***

I wasn't getting much sleep these days, so when I received the message that Eartha wanted to see me immediately, I wasn't surprised. Eartha, former Neo Astronaut and Delta's mother was a very personable leader. An attractive woman, whose fierceness was masked by her infectious smile, she was dedicated to the Planet's tenants and was the force of nature that restructured our planet's government. A tall woman with a statuesque presence, her dark brown, curly hair formed a halo over her head. She was an incredible organizer, a seer; but she evoked a tenderness and sensitivity to human life that the planet, in these times of rebirth desperately needed. Her heart and tenacity was now legendary. When they were trapped on Earth, it was Eartha that my father sent to make a go at flying beyond their solar system to our galaxy. She either sent her directives telepathically or requested a meeting in person. This one would be a face to face.

I liked Eartha. She is a thoughtful leader, but I wasn't in the mood for a lecture. My absence at the festival was local gossip. Not that Eartha cared about such things, but she did care about me. Or more importantly, she cared about her son's well-being, and therefore I was top priority.

We met in the Room of Love. What Earth's states of unity called the War Room, we called the Room of Love. A sunlit space station above the city's capitol building, where we could see out, but no one could see in, it had the most beautiful panoramic view of our refreshed cityskyline; and at night, one was literally amongst the stars.

The décor was all white and soft pink, and the cushions we used as chairs hovered above the marble. Eartha preferred to have her colleagues sit in lotus position during all meetings. She felt it helped focus the mind. A pink crystal mounted in a tree stump sat at the room's center. I was seated, legs folded on the floating cushion, my eyes closed in meditation. When I opened them, Eartha was seated across from me.Her body-hugging purple suit was a second skin that stretched her height; and she bore the Neo Astronaut pendant, a gold image of wings enshrouding our planet, on her chest. She sent a pitcher of steaming Purple Water my way, used her mind to direct the pitcher as it poured hot liquid into a tall glass. I took the cup's handle and she directed the pitcher to do the same for her, before gliding it to a small silver table with a large fuchsia book and white quill pen."You like attention, don't you?" Eartha said, with a toasty cheekiness that made me feel exposed.

"I needed some time away," I said. "I apologize if I offended you."

"It's not your absence from the festival that bothers me," Eartha said, taking a sip of the liquid and then commanding the cup to stand suspended. "It's your absence from the council, your absence from our work—your absence from this world."

"I'm always present at our meetings," I said, knowing full well that my mind was elsewhere. My focus was off. My questions still went unanswered.

"Have you been teleporting?" she asked.

"No," I said, surprised by the question. Teleporting wasn't exactly encouraged since our return, and the committee created to determine its function was, well, not functioning. We hadn't met in some time. No one, including myself, wanted to deal with it; and much of our travel focus was developed around the construction of smart, undetectable flying machines.

"The teleport project, as controversial as it maybe, is still a

worthy exploration," she added, "as is the time travel work that Moulan began. There is power in navigating space and time. And there's a way to incorporate it into our planet's tenants and lifestyle. There is a way to do this responsibly. Do you agree?" she asked.

"Teleporting, I believe, is a valuable, efficient way to travel," I said. "I don't know how the time travel element, the occupying of previous or future life, could be beneficial to the whole; although I think it's a worthy journey for the individual."

Eartha waited for me to say more. She straightened her back a bit, stretching the curve of her spine as she waited.

"I don't know if soul journeys can be mapped with procedure," I remarked. "I don't know how you would teach a teleporter to safely protect themselves from getting lost in time."

"I see," she said. "Let's take a walk," Eartha said.

After the rebirth, our master architects levied a host of feats. Among them was the mile-high skyway that circled our city. Encased in a see-through tube, citizens could walk the city skyway, yet another perspective on the town we'd built, preserved, and fought for. Planet Hope is a beautiful place. But even in this stellar trek through the heights of urban wonder, I still felt disconnected. Eartha was right, I wasn't here. I wasn't present.

"I can't claim to know how the world's turmoil impacted you," she said, as we strolled together through the skyway. "We all were changed in some way," she said. "But we all show up bringing the best of ourselves for our work in the present," she said, smiling warmly. Eartha towered over me, and her manner, though sunny, made me feel that I was being admonished like a child.

Eartha had such a sunny way about her directives that I couldn't stew in frustration. "I think you need to travel," she said. "You and Del ta should leave Planet Hope, go live near Earth's sun—Mars maybe or Titan. "You crave adventure," she said. "I'll give you assignments out that way." Travel? I stopped walking. Eartha took a few paces, noticed I was behind and stopped, too.

"Eartha, you don't have to make up things for me to do," I said plainly. "There's plenty to be done right here."

"Rayla, unlike your father and I, you have only known war. You don't know how to live in peace. I don't believe more Planet Hope procedural duties are the answer. You need to detox. You need a vacation. You need what others call normalcy."

"It's a little late for that," I quipped. A vacation—was she serious? "Anyplace but Earth," she said. "I've been all over that solar system. It's an interesting series of worlds. Bizarre but good people. Nice space stations. Plenty of fun. It's no Planet Hope, but I think you need something new. Something in the present. It's time you get to know who you are now. It's the Rayla of today that we need to help with Planet Hope of the future. I tried to appreciate the offer, but I was insulted. It was my ability to travel to other lives that got her and dozens of others back there. Now they wanted me to be in the present? What an oxymoron.

"I don't know," I added. Being in the present wasn't my issue. We continued walking together. The sun was high in the sky and the brilliant light danced off the windows, splintering the skyway into a prism of colors."It's an odd charge, I know," she said. "But how are you going to see your mother if you stay on this planet?" she added. Again I was stunned. Eartha wanted to provide me with an opportunity that my own father shunned. "Out there she'll find you." But I wouldn't be fooled.

"You just want to know what she's up to," I said, not falling for the bait. "That, too," Eartha said. "Although, I have an idea," she said. "But that is secondary. You are no good to me or to my son in your current state. Go off beyond the horizon. Have your own adventure and tell me about it." At that point, her craft arrived. She hopped on and flew off."

Chapter 3

Second Rock from the Sun

KENT slammed his fist on the dinner table, rattling the plates of vegetables that dotted the table. We were having our weekly dinner. He, Sui Lee, I and occasionally Delta, would meet each week at their home for a meal. It was our formalized way of reacquainting ourselves to this world and to one another. But our pleasantries were quickly eclipsed by our heated debates. All four of us had our own thoughts about Planet Hope, the meaning of life, the values of teleporting; and if we didn't watch the clock, we'd debate well into the next sunrise. But today it was just Dad, Sui Lee, and I. Delta would join us later, which was a good thing because Kent was piping mad over Eartha's new directive.

"I can't believe it," Kent said, his barrel chest heaved and his dark eyes widened with each heavy breath.

"It's not so bad," Sui Lee interjected, passing me a plate of carrots. "Rayla could use a refresher." Sui Lee's matter-of-factness was the yin to my father's yang. She tucked her black hair behind her tiny ears and sipped her hot tea through a straw.

"A refresher is one thing," added Kent. "But why there? Why that solar system? Of all the suns in this Milky Way, she sends her to the one where she could be apprehended."

"Kent, we know you're not exactly a fan of the region, and for good reason," said Sui Lee. Sui Lee stayed in Sebastion's Cave, praying to keep high consciousness for the people in the caves during the Neo Astronaut's absence. She disappeared into the cave when I was the rebel war strategist.

"But it is the only place we know of that has human life. That solar system is our homeland."

"I'm not a little girl, Dad," I said. He ignored me.

"And she's sending her son, too," Kent said. "She's trying to make contact. We specifically said that we were going to stay away from Earth until we determined how best to approach this matter of our being a myth. She's ignoring everything the council agreed to," Kent said, his temples popping with sweat. I never saw my dad so angry.

"She's sending too well deserving adults on a much needed vacation," said Sui Lee.

"Sui Lee, you know nothing about what's out there," he said.

"There are many things we don't know," Sui Lee added. "And many things we do." She looked to Kent and put her lips to her straw for another sip. "Rayla, what do you want?" Sui Lee asked, pouring another cup of tea.

"I'd like to go," I said in between chomping on carrots and spicy turnip greens. "I want to see how other worlds think and live. I think it would be good for me." Kent narrowed his eyes in disbelief.

"They only think one way…the way of Earth. Those planets are all Earth colonies and in the Galactic Conference. It's a trap and I will not have my daughter used as bait."

"I did live there in other lives," I said quietly.
Kent didn't respond.

"Kent, you know it's for the best. None of us have had Rayla's experience," Sui Lee chimed. "She's proved she can take care of herself. Otherwise, we, none of us would be here."

"Do what you must," he said. "Wisdom on this planet is obviously a thing of the past." Kent pushed himself away from the table and headed into his private room. I looked to Sui Lee. She nodded and I headed out to join my father.

Chapter 4

Who Told You You Could Rearrange Me?

MY father's fear was real. The solar system of our origins was a wily place. Moulan was out there. But Kent knew I could take care of myself. What did he think I'd find? Was it Moulan he feared or something else?

"Dad," I said, as I sat next to him on his aqua meditation mat. My father's meditations were so powerful I felt light-headed just stepping into the room. The sun was setting, but the red light streaming in from the window stretched across my father's chiseled face. He opened his eyes and squinted.

"What do you see?" I asked.

"I don't want to lose any more time. We've been separated long enough," he said.

"I won't be gone long," I said. I felt like a child—the child I didn't get to be with him when he was snatched away by the No Dirk. Then he was snatched away by Moulan.

"But who will you be when you return?" he responded. I nestled closer. There was some irony in the moment. Here I was longing to know more about my mother; and my father, who at one point was lost in time, was anchored beside me. I knew his love, but I didn't know him either. And I should.

"Kent, what's out there? What are you really afraid of?," I asked.

"You go out there. You make some friends. Live a life. Walking away isn't so easy. Some people don't let you go that easily. They stay with you, their thoughts clinging to you.They hold those memories so dear, it's like a cord through time. You're always connected. Do you want to create more of those kinds of relationships?" he asked.

"Isn't that life?" I asked. He didn't look at me but rather stared into the wall before us. Did he feel bound to Moulan? Was he talking about someone else?I couldn't ask. One day Dad would tell me about his years away from Planet Hope. One day he would tell me about Moulan. But today was not that day. He kissed me on the forehead.

"Avoid the sea," he said, changing the subject.

"What?" I said, as he dusted himself off and stood, towering over me.

"Avoid the sea. Those waters out there are strange repositories of love, fear, loss and peace. Strange things have happened in those waters. They're unexplored. Misunderstood. Avoid them. Do you promise?" he asked, his eyes aglow with concern. I stood. "Yes, I promise."

"If you go below the sea, I can't help you. Do you understand?" he asked.

"No, I don't," I retorted.

"Say yes," he said with a chuckle. "Just say yes. It will reassure me that the inevitable won't come upon us."

"Yes," I said, confused. Then his mood flickered.

"Well, when are you off?" he asked. "If I know Eartha, she's probably got you scheduled to leave this week."

"Tomorrow," I said. He chuckled. "Figures," he remarked and walked out the room.

***

The plans were all laid out. Delta and I would stay in Red City, a metropolis on Mars. Eartha, through her old connects, had arranged for us to stay in a tiny apartment in a crowded building where we wouldn't be noticed. Our contact was a guy named Jason, a professor who would check up on us. We were given Galactic IDs with fake names, a currency card for us to buy whatever we needed, and a tiny book on the history of Mars. My name would be Deb Donna. Delta would go by Atled, his name in reverse. Delta and I would be researchers on a project with Jason, giving us free reign to learn more about the world.

"Report what you find," Eartha said. "It's a world with many energy fields, and I would like to get your take on it. No pressure."
We would teleport there, making our arrival easier.
Luba decided to visit me my last day before the trip. Luba was enjoying her new Planet Hope life. Although she had her own crystal tent near the heart of the city, she preferred crashing with me. She couldn't stop talking about the wonder of Red City. She plopped down on my bed, her words dancing around me. I sat on the opposite end of the bed and watched.

"Everyone who's anyone goes to Red City," she says. Luba had never been. Her life on Planet Hope was her first time off the planet. She'd devoted her life to getting off Earth, a task made difficult by those not of the upper ranks. "It's the fast life. You're gonna have so much fun. And the men…."

"Well, I'm not going there for that," I said.

Luba looked around, as if there was someone in my place who could hear us.

"If I were you, I'd see if I could go alone. Leave Delta here and just live a little."

"Seriously, Luba?" I said.

Other men, really? If I thought about it too long, I'd wonder if Eartha just wanted to break Delta and me up. Delta and I had spent most of these new weeks post return with one another. We trusted one another fully. No one had gone through our time warp the way we had. Our bond was unexplainable, with a history as deep and abstract as our destined future. Delta was my right arm. I didn't have to think about loving him. I just did. After Carcine stayed behind on Earth, I didn't want to contemplate loving other men. It was all too much.

"See if you can take me instead of Delta," she squealed, her devilish smile lighting the room.

"No, Luba." She rolled over on my bed and laughed, staring me down.

"Do you ever think about him?"

"Who?" I asked, knowing full well whom she was talking about.

"Carcine. Do you ever wonder?"

"No, I don't, Luba." Luba was Carcine's girlfriend on Earth, a near shocker when I found him disconnected to the mission and disconnected to Planet Hope. Carcine was my first love. He was the true reason I wound up on a quest for the Neo Astronauts. He appeared in lifetime after lifetime; and by the time we reconnected as ourselves, he'd given up on Planet Hope. He gave up on me. Luba's inquiry was puzzling, but I guess it's talks like these that girlfriend/sisters are supposed to have. I honestly wouldn't know. She's my first woman friend.

"Do you miss him?" I asked. I didn't want to hear her answer. I didn't want the aching pain to return.

"Sometimes," she said. The conversation was getting weird. We both, at one point, loved Carcine. I loved him on one end of the time spectrum and she on the other. Here, she and I were together, and Carcine was a not-so-distant memory.

"We were such good friends," she said lightly. "He believed in me. But I would never go back," she noted, sitting again and rolling around on the bed in wistful remembrance.

"Why not?" I asked.

"There was no hope," she joked. "On Planet Hope you can live your dreams. Life isn't as complicated. People aren't eating away at your humanity," she said. Not now, I thought. Luba didn't understand that this new Planet Hope was a discovery for me, too.

"Are you surprised that Carcine didn't want to come back?" she asked, her eyes narrowing with curiosity.

I glared at Luba. Where was she going with this incredibly awkward conversation? But maybe that's the point. The conversation shouldn't be that awkward if I'd truly moved on. Apparently, she had.

"I thought he was dedicated to the tenets of Planet Hope. I thought he believed. But he didn't."

"Belief isn't for everyone," Luba said, sitting up and twirling her hot pink curls. "I believed there was more to life. That belief carried me in dark times when I was hungry and alone. It carried me when I danced with strange men. It carried me when there was no reason to believe I'd see another day. Now look at me. I'm in a palace in the stars." I didn't reply. I had a pink crystal on my desk and rolled it around in my palm. Luba continued.

"Carcine didn't believe in Planet Hope," Luba said cavalierly, sliding the comment in and looking away as if she hadn't said it."Carcine believed in you. You were Planet Hope." I stopped rotating the stone.

"I'm not saying you should have chosen Carcine," she said quickly, as if she were apologizing."If you don't want him, you don't want him. Obligation is no substitute for love." Luba's words were cutting me in two. I was simmering.

"Why are you angry?" she asked, her brown eyes popping with question marks.

"Because I'm trying to move forward," I said. My voice trembled a bit. "Isn't that what this life is about? Moving forward?"

"Life in my solar system isn't easy," she said. "People don't care for one another the way they do on Planet Hope. Your only protection is to be honest. Your connection to your thoughts and feelings in the present are all you have. Be your own anchor."

"There's a lot of delusion and wonder that way," she said. "Mars is mysterious. A lot of misery disguised as nostalgia and merriment. It can be so beautifully weird and delectable. Personally, I love it. I know it. But you don't."

"Maybe I should stay," I said, easing out my bed and trying to busy myself. But there was nothing to grab. Nothing to fiddle through to distract me from Luba's unearthing of my vulnerability. "You can't. But I'm sure you'll uncover a new mission," she cooed."A new mission that doesn't have anything to do with Planet Hope. A new mission all your own."

"What's this new mission?" I asked. "You seem to know so much," I added with a hint of sarcasm."Maybe you'll discover that you like living in the shadows," said Luba with a smile."Is that what you and Carcine did? You lived in the shadows?" I asked."No. He liked delusional merriment," she said. I wanted to tackle her. But I refrained, grabbed my crystal, and looked to the towers outside my window. Obama City was beautiful. But in my travels even I knew that home was relative. As I looked at the glistening towers, I knew that this Mars place would come to be home for me, too.

Chapter 5

No Fear in Freedom

THIS teleport would be a bit different than the last with Moulan. Delta and I stood at the center of Eartha Mandela's ebullient living room. Kent, Sui Lee, and Eartha stood before us. We weren't chanting very long when I could suddenly feel the lightness. Delta and I held hands. I could feel the flash of red engulf me. I could see the glistening red sands, the city of red, and the red dwellings. When I awakened, my room was a fuzzy blur of red. A handsome man with warm brown eyes and dark straight hair, clipped at the ears was sitting beside me. He wore a red top; fitted, shimmery pants; and red-rimmed glasses. Wow, that was fast.

"I'm Jason," he said with warm clarity. "Welcome to Red City."

***

I sat at a red steel table and gobbled up the bowl of spicy food Jason prepared for me in a kitchen of varying hues of, well, red. I could see the entire apartment from my chair. The walls were see-through. In fact, I could see everyone on the entire floor: A round woman in a short red dress was reading in a floating chair with no legs. Two teens in red tunics were arguing down the hall. Two thin men embraced in a dance below us. A short man with broad shoulders was taking a shower across the hall.

“Can they see me?” I asked

“Why yes,” Jason said. “I can turn off the viewing sensors if you like. But here in Red City we believe in living on the world stage. No need to watch fictitious shows when your neighbors are your entertainment,” he said.

“The couple downstairs has a knack for comedy that’s very old world Broadway,” he said. “That guy in the shower has the most beautiful singing voice in the morning. And the woman cooking next door has the best recipes. She makes a wonderful Jupiter Pasta. Red City residents stopped watching television and reading stories decades ago. Our own lives are more fascinating. But don’t worry. I turned off the censors in your sleeping quarters. No one saw you arrive.” I scanned the room—all hints of red, simple metallic furniture with clean lines. A large painting of Mars hung in the living room.

“Where’s Delta?” I asked.

“He went for a walk,” Jason said as he sat by me at the table. A walk? I guess Delta didn’t have the patience to be cooped up in this place. It was unusually tiny and entirely probing. Jason slid a small cup of red liquid my way.

“It’s a Mars Special. Builds your immune system up to ward off the effects of radiation. We drink it daily or you can take a pill. Some people like the rush of not taking it. Gives them a high but it’s best to take it everyday.” I doused the sweet drink down. I felt light-headed.

“Well, Jason, tell me what I need to know.”

“Don’t you want to relax a little? I can ask the neighbor to sing and boost the audio.”

“No, thanks,” I said.

“I’m Jason. I teach art at Lakshmi University. I’m a painter,” he said before pausing and staring.

"Forgive me for staring, but one second my room is empty and next thing you know two people appear. Amazing."

"Can anyone hear you?" I asked.
"I muted the sound," he said. No privacy? Did Eartha know about this? How do we stay below the radar on a planet with no privacy?

"How'd you meet Eartha?" I asked.

"I didn't," he said. My father did. He told me that if a woman named Eartha ever contacted our family that I was to respond immediately. He passed away some years ago. Amazing. You just don't expect things like this to happen. But that's the power of believing in the myth."
Yes, we were a myth in this galaxy. We of Planet Hope were a myth everywhere.

I'm a living myth. I might as well be a unicorn.

"I guess I should tell you about life here," he said. "As you can see, we're very much about being seen."

"Tell me about you," I asked, gobbling down my food as if I'd never eaten before. The tastes were familiar. The spices were the same peppers we used, as far as I could tell.

"Like I said, I'm a teacher. I teach art. I grew up in Red City. My father was a pilot. That's how he met Eartha," he said before resorting to his staring and shaking it off. "I'm doing research on mythology. As I mentioned, we've completely lost the value of traditional storytelling. Everyone lives reality as fantasy. We used to totally be into virtual reality, but people craved authenticity. Anything old is quickly discarded around here, unless it's a fashion trend. At first it was trendy to dismiss history, but we've been doing it so long that no one here seems to know anything. Most kids today don't know that we originally came from Earth. They think human life has always been on Mars," Jason said with a sigh. "Mars is such a mystery. I mean, humans have lived here for two centuries or so, but we're pretty clueless about what happened before. I mean, it was a wasteland for the most part. But there are myths that people lived here once before, too. That's what I investigate."

"Do you believe them?" I said in between mouthfuls.

"You appeared. I might as well," he said. "It makes for great storytelling and art if nothing else. Somebody's got to preserve this stuff. Might as well be me."

It was a worthy pastime, I thought. Jason watched me as I munched on. He was very inviting. From the looks of it he lived alone, and I didn't get the impression he had many friends. He was happy to see us. We affirmed some of his research, I assumed.

"I think something lived here before," Jason said. "Whether they were human or not is a completely different story. But thousands, millions of years ago this planet had water. Most of the water we have now we created in the past two centuries, but there's proof of old rivers and lakes that were dried up. And there's one pool of water that's deep below the crust. I found it a few years ago.

"You found it?" I said, somewhat surprised. So he's a scientist, too?

"When I'm not painting, I'm a diving hobbyist, you could say. I bum around. But it's such a complicated process getting down there. The water hasn't been explored.It's hard to get people to go with me. They're too busy looking at one another in their apartments and at work.

"It's an alternative water source," I said.

"Maybe," Jason said. "Or there could be life."
Jason pulled out an old tattered thick book. I flipped through it. There were images of curvaceous women with big hair and fins.

"They're Mermaids," he said. "Half-human, half-fish." They've lured sailors on Earth. Some people think they're the great human ancestor, for some of us anyway." I'd heard the stories before.

"You think there are Mermaids beneath the surface?" I said.

"Yes," he said. The door slammed. Delta walked in.

"Is everything in this town red," he yammered in disgust. "Everything?"

"It's the Red City," Jason said quietly, not wanting to offend his guest.

"No kidding," Delta chimed. He took a seat. "What would happen if I wore blue?"

"The law says we wear, red," Jason said.

"You got any other crazy laws besides the fact that everyone can see everything?," Delta asked.

"A couple," Jason said.

"I need another nap," Delta said, pushing himself away from the table. The drag of the chair looming in the air. He headed to his bedroom and shut the door.

"These trips can be disorienting, I suppose," said Jason meekly. "And he didn't take too well to the Mars Special."

"No, he's doing just fine." I said. I looked to Jason's painting of the Red Planet.

"Did you paint this?" I asked.

"No, I bought it. My work is in my studio," he said. He filled my cup with more of the Martian Special. "You might as well have another?" he asked. But instead of dousing it down, I watched as Jason poured his. He held up his tea cup for a toast. "To your visit. May the discoveries be enchanting. Enchanting is a word they say in myths and fables all the time. I like saying it," he said with a winners smile. "En chanting. Yes, may we all be enchanted," I said and drank up.

***

Delta and I slept in separate beds. The censors were turned off so no one could see us, which was good because Delta was having a flippant fit.

"I don't like this place," Delta said.

"You've only been here a few hours," I said.

"I don't like it. I don't like these see-through walls. I don't like the people. I don't like the energy fields. The conflicting energy fields keep everyone frenetic, like they're loose electric wires or nuclear reactors," he added. "I walked around outside and it was like dancing around radiation currents. I'm an outdoors guy and the atmosphere out here is nothing like anything I've experienced. How long do we have to be here?"

"At least a few weeks," I said. Delta turned on his stomach and closed his eyes.

"I don't like it," he said and drifted off to sleep.

***

The following day, Jason took us to the university. He gave us a tour. The entire city was a mix of reddish caves and skyscrapers. The university itself was shaped like a giant dome. The students were pretty rambunctious. I could see what Delta meant. The energy fields were enigmatic. Everyone zipped about and talked at a rapid speed. They had a litany of wired devices plugged into their arms, their ears. They were communication devices, but it appeared that everyone was always talking to someone, but never the person in front of them. Jason said it was the wired life, a trend to imitate the early 21st century.

"All the kids are really into it," he said. "Makes teaching a bit difficult, though." Jason took us into his art gallery. His works, as you could imagine, were all red. He showed us more paintings of Mermaids and Mermen that he'd collected. He let us listen to a few accounts of Mermaid spottings from the old world on his recording device. "Let me get this straight," Delta said, still in his flippant mood. "You want us to look for women with gills?"

"It's just an idea," Jason said. "You can explore it metaphorically if you like." Jason was very enthusiastic about this myth of water people below the crust, but I didn't share his excitement. I remembered my father's warning about the water, and I was shocked to find myself confronted with the amorphous lake so soon into our journey. Delta's reckless mood wasn't helping."There's a different energy field underground, too. The radiation levels are virtually nonexistent," Jason said.

"Take us to the lake and we'll dive down there ourselves," Delta said.

"Really?" Jason said.

"Yes, let's get this thing going. If there are women out here with fins on, I want to see them. And I need a change of environment immediately."

"Delta," I said. "I think we need a special clearance. I think we're just supposed to investigate and collect myths, right?" I said, looking to Jason.

"Forget that," Delta said. "I want to see. I need to see something besides Red and these radiation-fried people."

"You don't need clearance," Jason said.

"We're trying to stay low profile," I added gently. "I thought you wanted adventure?" Delta said? "Get me in those waters and I'll go as deep as you want."

"This is wonderful," Jason said. Had Delta gone mad? I thought about my promise to my father. Stay away from the seas. Do underground ancient lakes count? Something about the whole notion made me feel alive, though. More alive than I'd felt in some time. I used to live beyond the edge. What was this fetish I was having with safety? It must be the sedated peaceful life of comfort that was closing me in. Is that what I missed? Was this the life in the shadow Luba was talking about? "Yeah, I'll go, too," I said. Jason smiled. "Good thing I have extra scuba gear."

***

After leaving the university, I left Jason and Delta to walk around the city alone. Everywhere in this town was jam packed with people. It was a marvel that they could think at all. The market was teaming with merchants and buyers. People shoved and pushed, yelled and yammered. Most of the buildings were see-through, and I could see the mundane activities of Martian life through their apartment and office walls. I thought about the people in Sebastian's Cave, but those people were tepid and quiet. This world of people was loud and vivacious. I wandered about. The fruit was interesting. Apparently, they created their own fruit and foods, all red of course. "Rayla," a man's voice called. I turned about. It was Cheyenne, the traveler from Chicagotropolis that I met with Delta and Luba. Tall and stunning, he took a bite of his red apple and tossed it to the ground. "You made it," he said. "I knew you were pulling my leg with that Planet Hope thing. You're a Mars girl. Should've guessed it. I'm just in town visiting family. What are you doing these ways?" I was too stunned to speak. Never did I expect to see anyone I knew. What a small universe. "Just checking out the market," I said with a smile. "You got out of dodge just in time. Shortly after we met, there was some big catastrophe at club Rhiannon. All kinds of crazy ghost spottings and flying people. It was crazy. The government had the whole lot of it quarantined. It was getting a little out of pocket for me, so I just came here.""What happened?," I said quietly, knowing full well the war of the Shangos, Neo Astronauts, Moulan, and more that took place."Too many stories to figure out," he said. The flying people did me in. I doubled over when I heard that one. Never did find the owner, Carcine. There's some crazy story about him walking into the sea and becoming, get this, a Merman. People in Chicagotropolis lost their doggone nuggets, I tell you. Can't tell fact from fiction.""A Merman?""You heard me right," he chimed. "Anyways,we should meet up sometime." I'm going on vacation on Titan for a few; but when I return, let's get up. Bring that friend of yours, too. You guys still together?" I was still stunned. "Well anyways, here's my info. Call me sometime." Cheyenne handed me a card and disappeared into the sea of red citizens.

Chapter 6

Blue Moon

CARCINE'S a Merman. I lay in my bed staring at the ceiling. I must be dreaming. I thought of Kent and his offhanded comments about the strings of time—people holding on to you. Was Carcine holding on to me? Was I holding on to him?

I didn't want to tell anyone. I could only imagine Delta's reaction. Jason would be elated. I felt like reaching out to Luba.
I shook it all off. Even if Carcine was a Merman, he wouldn't be here on Mars, I reasoned. I should just keep this to myself, explore the waters, and live the Martian life. But that would never happen.
When Delta and Jason returned I told them everything. Their reactions were as expected.

"You will find your man," Delta said with a snicker. I ignored him.

"This is amazing," Jason said. It seemed to be the only word he could find to explain me, Delta, and his theory of Mermaids.

"We must go to Chicagotropolis and explore," he said. "We need to collect stories, interview people."

"We're not going to Earth," I said calmly. "We'll explore the waters here and if you want to go to Chicagotropolis without us, you should," I said.

"I suppose you're right," Jason said quietly. "It would be dangerous for you."

"I live for danger," Delta yammered. "Think I'll go for another walk," he said and left the apartment.

***

Several hours had passed and Delta had not returned. Jason made dinner for me. He yearned to know more about Planet Hope. I told him everything. He was spellbound.

"It sounds like a marvel of a place," he said. "Why come here?" I told him about Eartha's directive and he listened eagerly.

"My dad said she was a wonderful person," he said, nostalgia waxing his eyes. He missed his father. For a moment, I missed mine.

"Why are you so curious about these Mermaids?" I asked.

"My father claims he saw one," Jason said. "He lost contact with control, was flying over the human-made waters of Mars,and landed on the water waiting to regain contact. He opened the hatch and sat atop the vehicle to get some fresh air when he saw a Mermaid come out of the sea. She asked him if he was well, if he needed anything. She knew his name and invited him to go below. My dad said he was completely mesmerized, but he couldn't do it. He feared that he would never return," Jason said.

"Then he doubted his senses. These were human-made waters. Why would Mermaids be there?" Jason said. He must have shared this story with Eartha. "I can understand if you're hesitant to go below the sea," Jason said."You don't have to do it for me. Delta and I can go alone." Jason was right. I didn't have a point to prove. "Thank you, Jason. Thank you." I hugged him and headed off to my bedroom.

Chapter 7

Red Dirt People

"I'm a dirt person. I trust the dirt. I don't trust diamonds and gold.
- Eartha Kitt

JASON spent a day or so showing us how to use the deep sea diving equipment. It was fairly simple. I had decided not to go below the sea, but I would accompany them to the cave where this still water nestled. Apparently, Mars was anarchist, said Jason. They had no true government, a livelihood that the Martian people protected fiercely. The lake was in the former Forbidden Zone, an area with high radiation levels that were diminished a decade ago. While it was free and open to all who felt like coming out there, Jason said that the area was rural and simply not sexy enough for the Martian people. "It's deserted," he said.

We took a hovercraft over. Delta and I had an opportunity to view the rural Martian terrain, a landscape of red soil and craters. Jason landed us at the bottom of the Canyon of Gods, a canyon as deep as it was wide. There was a large hole four times as large as our craft at the bottom. Jason said that we would have to climb down. "It's about 100 meters," he said. "The sea is at the bottom."

The sun was high in the sky so we had adequate light. Jason affixed a rope ladder to the base of the canyon as a climbing option. But there was a rocky stairway that we could walk down, too. Jason led the way with Delta and I following. We had lightweight backpacks and watched our step as we walked to the bottom. At the base of the pit, Jason turned on the flashlight. We followed him through a narrow corridor and on the opposite side the underground sea awaited us. The sea was in a giant canyon 100 or so meters high, but it extended as far as the eye could see. Jason had affixed a few lights in the canyon during his first visit, and those floodlights were all we needed to see the infinite stretch of the sea. Delta began adjusting his deep-sea diving gear and Jason did the same.

"It's beautiful isn't it?" Jason asked.

But I maintained my war trained eye, scoping out the perimeter. It wasn't beautiful at all. This water had another purpose. But what? Jason and Delta tightened their gear. I found a flat surface a meter from the water's edge and sat with my legs crossed. This ancient pool had memory, a story. It reminded me of something, but with the rush of the moment I couldn't recall what it was. Delta looked out to the water.

"No one else comes out here, huh?" Delta asked.

"No," Jason added, adjusting his gear.

"Well, they used to a long, long time ago," Delta strapped his goggles over his eyes.

"You ready?" he asked Jason. Jason nodded. Delta turned to me. "If we're not back in an hour, you know what to do," he said.

For a moment I thought of Carcine and his three-day trek to find Moulan that evolved into eternity. "If I'm not back in three days, find Moulan," he said. When he didn't return, it was I who found her and he would be lost to me forever." I pushed the thought out of my mind.Delta and Jason dove in and within seconds they were gone. I sat in the cave and looked about. The silence was a power all its own. I closed my eyes for a moment and a thought flashed so quickly I opened them immediately. This was no ordinary cave. I knew this place like the pulsing of my own heartbeat. It was as close as breath and as distant as the furthest star. Could it be? I looked at the dark stone with its hints of red, and the sparkles emerged. This was the Crystal Cove. But was it the Crystal Cove of my journey in East Africa? Was it the Crystal Cove of my dreams? Was it the one that restored me in Vietnam? Would it lead to the makeshift one created in Chicagotropolis? I stood, startled by my forgetfulness. I hadn't thought about the cove since my return. I hid its power deep within, almost fearful that the reconnection would take me away from the rebuilding of Planet Hope. I feared the teleport, feared the time travel, and like the rest of my planet, pushed it into the far recesses of my mind for the purpose of fitting in with our new normal.

I spun around studying the walls, and there embedded in the stone were tiny turquoise crystals. I gasped. I looked to the water. The Crystal Cove, the Crystal Cove…I kept repeating it in my mind. I felt so out of touch. The Crystal Cove had been a source of life, rejuvenation; and I had completely forgotten about it. But why was there water here? Then it struck me so powerfully I stumbled and caught myself before tumbling over. The Crystal Cove was a portal and this sea was a portal. I thought of my lives with the Crystal Cove, and each one was near a body of water.

How could I have forgotten? Were all these coves connected? Was there a portal of seas that connected oceans and lakes across the universe? Were these bodies of water home of the Mermaids and Mermen of the greatest fiction of our time? I couldn't wait an hour. I scanned the surface of the clear sea looking for answers. I needed to tell them. Should I wait? Should I dive in? Why hadn't I thought of this before? My father's promise reverberated in my mind; but before I could repeat his warning, I dug into my backpack and slipped into the oil slick clothing and oxygen tank. I saw my reflection in the pool and dived in to greet her.

The water was crystal clear. If I moved quickly enough, I should see them I figured. There was scant marine life. Some algae, some coral, but I wasn't looking to be immersed in beauty. I hovered just below the surface to give myself a bird's eye view. The sea creatures grew larger as I moved on, and the underwater vegetation brightened. I continued moving along, keeping my breathing steady and my focus narrow.

Just as doubt was about to creep in, I saw them a few meters below me. But the shock of the spotting nearly halted my flow. I quickly regained my breathing. Yes, that was Jason and Delta below. But they weren't wearing their diving clothes. They looked my way and swam with cheerful smiles. What were they doing? I thought. But they didn't have shirts and they were affixed to a fishtail. They swam toward me with unprecedented speed. "Rayla, you don't need those clothes. Take them off," Delta said. His voice was as clear as it would be above water. I shook my head. Jason circled me.

"You get instant fins down here," Jason said. I shook my head again and sent Delta a powerful thought wave. Delta received it. "She says this is a time portal," Delta told Jason. The water didn't affect his speech and he breathed with the ease of a salamander. "It could lead to anywhere."

"Let's head back," Jason said. A light ebbed from the distance. All three of us could see the green glow on our arms. The glow flashed at the rate of a heartbeat. I looked to the distance and saw a green Sphinx mounted at the bottom. Two Mermaids, one with black curls the other with wavy red hair circled the edifice.

"We should go," I messaged to Delta. But Delta was swimming towards them. "Delta," I cried as he swam on. Jason looked to me and back to Delta and followed behind him. I wanted to turn around, but the familiar voice of syrup enclosed me.

"Rayla, you've found me," Moulan's voice echoed. "I knew you would find me, my sweet." My tense body relaxed. My will was succumbing to Moulan's. I resisted.

"It's okay," she said. "Come to me. You'll be fine."

"Delta," I cried. He turned for a moment.

"Rayla, we're home," he said, completely overcome by the power of Moulan.

"Delta," I cried in my mind. "Remember Planet Hope."
With that, Delta jerked and turned to me with a look of nostalgic confusion. He shook off the mesmerism, grabbed Jason by the arm, and swam with all his might toward me. We moved as swiftly as their fins and my flippers would take us.

"Don't leave," Moulan said soothingly. "Don't leave."

"Don't leave," a man's voice bellowed. But I wouldn't turn around.

I knew that voice. I knew Carcine's voice anywhere. Within moments we were back to our starting point. I pulled myself out the lake. As the men pushed themselves up, their fins disappeared. They grabbed their back packs and we moved swiftly through the corridor and flew up the steps. We hopped into the craft. Jason fired up and we were on our way back to Red City. All of us were silent. But when we hit the outskirts of the city, I found the words to speak.

"All the lakes of the universe are aligned," I said. "There are underwater cities that trek across the universe."

"It's a whole new world," Jason said. Delta was the last to speak.

"I almost never came back," he said. He spoke barely above a whisper. "I've never felt so at peace in my life." I didn't know what to make of Delta's remark. What did he mean? As we neared Jason's apartment, we noticed a host of black hovercrafts surrounding it.

"Why are the galactic police here?" he asked. I leaped to the controls and turned on the silent detector to cloak our presence.

"They're looking for us," I said. Jason circled back in the opposite direction.

"What do we do?" Jason asked.

"We may have to take you to Planet Hope," I said.

"Or we can go back to the sea," Delta responded.

"Yes, the sea," Jason echoed, almost lost in his own thought. At that moment, I focused all my energy on encapsuling our hovercraft.

"Rayla," Delta yelled. The hovercraft began to tremble. I must do it now, or we would never go back. I wrestled all control. I thought of Obama City, I thought of Kent and Sui Lee. I thought of freedom and the rebuilding of my home. I felt the shift. We must leave now and these men were coming with me. Jason yelled. But my home was Planet Hope. Home is where the heart is.

Chapter 8

The Liquid Life

"New World Water Make the Tide Rise High" - *Mos Def*

I awakened in my bed on Planet Hope. The sunlight streaked in through the window and adjacent balcony, tickling me with the glow of morning. Luba was at my side with a cup of tea. I motioned to speak, but she put her fingers to her lips and put the tea cup to mine. "When you're ready, everyone's waiting," she said. She mashed her lips to my ear and whispered. "And that Jason guy is really cute."

It didn't take long to freshen up. I forgot to ask Luba who "everyone" was. But when I stepped outside my door it became apparent. Eartha, Kent, Sui Lee, several Neo Astronauts, and the leading members of the council, along with Luba, were in my living room.

"What is this?" I asked.

"What did you do to my son?" Eartha asked.

"What?"

"My son. I looked to my left and there stood a large water tank with Delta inside, part man, part fish, he was trapped but unusually enthusiastic.

"Rayla, tell them to take me back to the Martian Waters. I've found my true home," he squealed with a happiness that belied his identity. Delta was not the cheery type.

Everyone stood and looked at me. I spotted Jason sitting alone at my tea table. Eyes bright, he leaned back in his seat, legs squared and smiled. His perkiness nearly matched Delta's.

"Who is this man?" Eartha yelled, pointing her long finger to Jason.

"Jason, your contact," I said.

"This is not Jason," she said with a terse calm. Jason looked to me and shrugged.

"Who are you?" I asked.

"I'm Jason," he said. "I'm a future myth as well, and I'm happy to be home."

"Home," I repeated.

"It's a bit hard to explain, but I'll say it plainly. I'm the last descendant of the original people of Planet Hope—an Original Original, you could say. You are not our planet's first citizens. I've come to reclaim my home," he said. "I don't want much, just a dwelling and a seat on the council."

"Why didn't you say this before?" I asked.

"Would you have believed me?" he asked.

"And what happened to Delta," I asked?

"He found his home. But Eartha knows more about that than I do, I'm sure." Eartha bit her lip.

"I would like to tell my story," Jason said.

"We would like to hear it," I said.

"We'll meet in my chambers," Eartha said, forcing restraint in her voice. She used her brain waves to lift Delta's tank and he floated out as the others filed out. Jason didn't move but Eartha gave him a look so commanding that he hopped to his feet and followed. My father, Sui Lee, and Luba stayed behind.

"You went below the waters didn't you?" Kent asked. I tried to explain but he cut me off.

"You resisted the Sphinx," he chimed. "Impressive."

"And she found Jason," Sui Lee said.

"I thought he was a myth," Kent added.

"Apparently not," Sui Lee said.

"We'll see you in Eartha's chambers," Kent said as he and Sui Lee slipped out the door.

Luba and I were alone. She swayed back and forth and began swooping her arms in circles as she danced between the chairs and couches in the tiny room.

"Did you get to have any fun?" she cooed, bouncing her hips slightly before spinning and twirling her arms. "None at all," I affirmed, taking a seat at the long white couch that once stretched across Delta's old lair. My Delta was mesmerized by the Martian Waters and this Jason character was rewriting our Planet's History with his very arrival. I prayed that Delta wasn't lost to me forever. There was a new past to be revealed in tandem with our new future. If the Galactic Authorities were on our tail we wouldn't be a myth for long. The seclusion that Planet Hope thought they could relish in was likely coming to a close.

If Jason's story were true, there might be others who can claim Planet Hope as their home. I'd never thought about others inhabiting this planet, and I was eager to hear Jason's story. I looked to my shelf and saw Moulan's Book bound and neatly squared. I was afraid to read the pages. Afraid I would be sucked into its words, much like I was almost sucked into the Sphinx. But at least I knew where she was. We would meet again. Besides, Delta at some point would have to go home. How the seas were his home would soon be revealed.

Luba stopped her circle motions and watched me. She darted to the tea table, poured a cup of white tea and sat beside me.
"Jason is really cute," she added. "Is he with anyone?"

"I don't think so," I said.

"You brought him for me, didn't you?" I laughed.

"Is that all you can think about at a time like this?" I asked. Delta was a Merman, for goodness sake. But I smiled to myself. For some odd reason, I wasn't bothered either.

"I'm not from this planet," she said with a giggle. "Your politics have nothing to do with me." I shook my head.

We clinked our tea cups and enjoyed the quick quiet moment as we watched the sunset. In a few moments I would be in Eartha's Chambers. I was used to the swift shifts of the universe and I wasn't bothered. No, I wasn't bothered at all.

NOMMU DREAMS

5

Chapter 9

Kronosaurus Rising

TENSION blanketed Eartha's off-pink chambers. The Room of Love, as we called it, was percolating with spider silk tapestries. I was the last to enter; and all eyes, as usual, were on me when I arrived. I was beginning to think that the Neo Astronauts didn't care for me very much. They sat coolly in their white ornate chairs at the floating rose-colored horseshoe of a table of the council. Eartha sat at the head and followed my movements closely, narrowing her eyes as I slid into my seat. This wasn't my fault but it might as well have been. The Neo Astronauts, my dad included, seemed to view me as an outsider whose actions had bizarre consequences; Jason's arrival and Delta's Mermaid status were among them.

Jason sat at the center of our circle of questions, his hands neatly folded on a desk in front of him. His calmness belied the swirl of confusion everyone kept bottled at the base of their throats. He was alert, his eyes were sharp, and his lips parted slightly for a winner's smile. Jason leaned back in his hot pink chair, crossed one leg over the other, and wrapped one arm around the chair's back. This was his world, it seemed, and we'd encircled him, hoping to glean truth from the words to come. If Jason was in fact an original citizen of Planet Hope, his presence changed everything. Nothing in our history said anything about Planet Hope having inhabitants before Earth's people set course and made it home. If Jason's words were true, we were invaders, not discoverers. We were, in some ways, the very thing our society was designed not to be—a people who conquered and had no regard for life. If Jason's soon to be revealed story was true, the rise of Planet Hope was the death of another way of life—our heroes not so heroic, our valor mired in inhumanity.

Jason wasn't bothered by our steady gaze and his easy demeanor contrasted the restrained Neo Astronauts who were teetering on the unhinged. Who was this man? I looked to Delta who swam around in a fish tank in the corner. He was so happy flitting about that he hardly noticed us. His silver tail lapped and water splashed over the rim. I had to bite my lip to keep from snickering. I wanted to laugh but I dared not.

Nothing about this moment was funny, although it was bizarre. Eartha raised a finger to begin the meeting and I felt like snickering again. There was no bringing order to this chaos."Introduce yourself," she said firmly.

"Like I said, my name is Jason," he said, his dark eyes sparkling under the soft pink light above. He pushed a few strands of his black hair out of his face. "I am the last of the true people of Planet Hope. Your early invaders forced my life form off the planet."

Lagos, the methodic wise fighter of the bunch leaned in, cracking his knuckles as he spoke.

"There's no record of anyone living on Planet Hope when our first astronauts arrived," he said in his trademark deep voice. Lagos was the one who spotted my cover in an old bar in the U.S capitol in 1970s America. He could snoop out anything.

"And why would there be?" Jason asked. "Your mission was to recreate a new Earth. You weren't exactly looking to cohabitate with other life forms."

"There were no records of any life forms," Lagos continued, his voice deepening.

"Your science wasn't so sophisticated. You relied too heavily on sight and the familiar," Jason quipped.

"Go on, Jason," Eartha urged firmly.
"More of your people came," Jason said. "You ignored us. You overlooked us. We went underground. We lived underground until those red soldiers of yours began digging tunnels. And then we did the unthinkable. We became fireflies," Jason said. He paused, forcing us to hang on to his every syllable.

Fireflies? What was this guy talking about?

"You did have a lot of early reportings of lightening bugs," he said.

"They were all over the place," Kent said. "I remember seeing some as a child myself. Ice wrote about them in her chronicles."
"All that light gave you hope," Jason said. "Thus the term Planet Hope. That's how we disguised ourselves. But even lightening bugs couldn't withstand your pollutants."

"I can't help but reiterate that there were no reports of humans when we arrived," Lagos echoed. Lagos was growing uncharacteristically angry. He swallowed the fire. "This man is lying."

"Who said anything about being human," Jason snapped.
"Just to be clear, your people never formally approached ours. You just assumed that we didn't want to cohabitate?" I asked.

"If you can't cohabitate with fireflies, how are you going to cohabitate with complex beings like us? We have the ability to take on any form we choose. Obviously, I'm choosing to take on this human form to make myself presentable for you."

"And what is your natural form?" I asked.

"We prefer to go without form," Jason said, looking me squarely in the eye. I felt something familiar with Jason. I felt a connection. Did I know him? Had we met in another time? Another place?

"Your natural state is invisible?" Diva asked in disbelief, bending forward and clasping her hands. Diva's feisty testiness could not be calmed by the hues of pink. A genius woman with piercing sarcasm, her cynicism was insightful and disarming. I liked her but she didn't care for me much, although she'd never admit it.

"Without form is not invisible," Jason quipped. "You should know that by now." Diva was unnerved. She took a breath.

"Let me be clear. Are you saying your people can't be seen with the naked eye?" Diva asked.

"It's your choice of the word 'people' that's the problem. We are beings. Formless beings," Jason reiterated.

"If you can go without form, how did we, our people, force you off the planet?" I asked.

"The beauty of our planet was the invisibility of life. We all existed quite happily in the potentiality of life. It was a precious state of eternal innocence and bliss. A rousing awareness of possibility and completion," he said with a sigh of nostalgia. "Three-dimensional existence wasn't necessary. You cultivated 3D life where none was needed," Jason added. "You terraformed to recreate what you already had instead of appreciated life as it was."

"Then how was our arrival the beginning of your end?" I asked.

"We took form—first the fireflies, later as humans. Others became blades of grass, h2O. We all took on form to adapt. But as we changed form, the culture changed and we were diminished. There was no more peaceful living in the formless. Either take form or don't exist. Can you imagine how destructive that was to our reality?" Jason asked, his forearms now rested on his square thighs. "Being forced to take form for survival was near hell. It was the death of us. We became splintered, fractured parts of a whole that may never reconnect."

"So you didn't function as individuals, you functioned as one?" Kent asked. He was puzzled. We all were.

"Correct," Jason said.

The Neo Astronauts all looked at one another.

"There were records of incredibly high energy fields and life sources when our first arrivers came to this land," said Sui Lee. "Planet Hope always

had incredibly high energy fields. I suppose that was you and your life forms?"

"Yes," Jason said. "And I'm sure your science will show your energy field weakened as the years rolled on," he said.

"True," Kent added.

"And it was our absence that contributed to your wobbling in space. Our absence made it easier for that witch of a scientist you all loved so much to navigate the realm of the formless. She no longer had us to deal with us. Didn't you ever wonder how she amassed so much power so quickly?"

The room was quiet. The Neo Astronauts were speechless. Everything Jason said made sense. It was completely unprovable. But now what? I looked to Delta splashing haplessly.

"I don't understand why you felt coerced to take on form," Kent asked.

"Two things can't occupy the same space at the same time," Jason said. "Technically," he added. We were dumfounded.

"Look, I don't have to debate the merits of living in form or life in the formless. It is what it is. I have adjusted for my own survival," Jason said. His cavalier cool only punctuated everyone's bewilderment.

"And how many of you became human?" I asked.
"Just a handful. Just those of us who went to Earth and later Mars. Others became comets, stars, light particles, cats."

"Tell us your story," Eartha continued.

"I lived as a firefly for some time and then a few of us rode your strings in Shogun City to Earth. We landed in a land called Mexico and became human. We lived in the city. I decided to be a boy, the others became a father, a mother. Two became women and married. We figured out your system of family order and mimicked it, hoping to just mix in. We worked at a data center for a few years and then took a ship off to Mars. My dad really bought into the human life. He was rather intrigued by the challenge of it all. He became a pilot and that's where he met you, Eartha. But you triggered something in him, and he decided to go back to formless living.

"He said you told him a story about a girl and a golden brick road; at the end you said 'There's no place like home.' It stuck with him and he left us. The others followed."

"And you didn't," I asked. "Why not?"

"To be honest with you, I just became really fascinated by this Mermaid myth thing. I mean, half of these stories are about the duality that the formless feel when they take form. I think the roots of these stories are incredible, and maybe I was hoping to get a better understanding of myself. I mean, how many formless cultures are out in this universe wrestling with the three-dimensional? How many more people are there like me, who came into this life purely by circumstance or invasion? How many want an out but are too wrapped up in the 3D to claim their true selves?"

Jason was pouring his heart out to us, and his eyes darted from one council member to the next but we had no answers. The notion of there being formless lives that we, in populating our planet, somehow completely ignored didn't sit well with our beginning story. Planet Hope citizens were respectful of life. But nothing in our consciousness gave much thought to life in the invisible.

"Question my existence if you want," Jason said. "I am a myth, but then again so are you."

"And if your story is true," Eartha added calmly. "How do we know you are one of the originals and not just some infatuated story-teller." Jason tilted his head. "I'm not one for magic tricks, Eartha. You'll just have to trust me."

"Why is my son a Merman?" Eartha said with the firmness of a mother scorned. She stood, floated to the center of the room, and planted herself before Jason, towering over him like a great maple over a stump. But Jason wasn't rattled.

"Maybe that's his original state," Jason said warmly, leaning so far back in his chair that the front legs were lifted. "All I ask is for a seat on the council and a place to call home. I'll go back and forth between Mars as needed."

"You will not hold my son hostage," Eartha screamed.

"I'm not doing anything," Jason said. "Look at him."

Delta kept flipping away. A bit more water splashed onto the chamber floor. Kent stood and rushed over to Eartha. He whispered something in her ear.

"Look, as a firefly I saw a lot of things that you Hopers were into," Jason continued. "You did a lot of experimentation. Some of you had some unique origins—hybrid DNA, cloning, everlasting 3D life. I can understand abandoning traditional means of creating life. As a formerly formless one, I just don't get why life is so complicated for you. It must be the gravitational pull. But when you make one woman the mother of everybody, it gets sticky."

One mother?

"That's enough," Eartha said. "You're excused."
Jason flashed a grin, stood, and moved on. Before he shut the chamber door, he glanced my way.

"You have no reason to believe me," Jason said, almost as an afterthought. "But you should." With that, he left the room.

Chapter 10

Water Wading

I took to the same hot pink seat and reported on all that happened on Mars. I shared my theory about the interconnected waterways, but my discovery paled in comparison to Jason's revelations. Although I was asked a few questions, most of the discussion was about the merit of Jason's claims.

"I believe him," Diva said. The cynic was a believer.

"Regardless of whether we believe him or not, the pressing question is what do we do now?" Eartha asked.

"I think whether we believe him or not is an important question," Kent said. "It says as much about us as it does about him. Are we mimicking the arrogance of our ancestors and assuming that we are the only life around?"

"Moulan said that we were the only life. She said that the other planets were just repositories for other lifetimes. Our world could be built on a space designed for other life in the making…perhaps a life that hasn't lived yet," I said.

The others mumbled.

"Moulan said many things and we can't give credence to all of it," Eartha added. Why were they acting as if Moulan's work meant nothing? Granted, she took it too far but there's something to her research. But no one wanted to talk about Moulan, ever.

"Why can't we just give him a seat on the council and a place to stay like he asked?" I said. Despite the shock of it all, I really didn't think his request was that big of a deal.

"There are too many questions. Is he a threat to our survival? Can he communicate with the other formless ones?" Lagos asked, his voice swallowing the room. "Perhaps they're all here, in their various states of existence waiting for his arrival."

"So that they can do what, become formless again?" I asked.

"What if he's trying to take over?" Lagos added.

"Then we'll have to figure out a way to coexist, like we should have done in the beginning," I added.

"How were our first arrivers supposed to negotiate with the formless? That's a preposterous assumption," Eartha said. "They made no contact."

"It's our whole notion of defining life that's the problem," I said. "In the early years was there any discussion as to whether we should inhabit this planet? The only life we acknowledged was plant life and the potential to sustain human life, but maybe this planet didn't have human life for a reason. Surely, Ice said something about this," I said, referring to our first griot and spirit guide.

"It was a choice," Diva added.

"My read on him indicates that everything he says is true," said Sui Lee. Sui Lee sat with her eyes closed the entire meeting.

"And there we have it. We know what he wants," Kent added.

"What do we want?"

After some discussion, the council decided to give Jason an advisory seat on the council. He would be introduced to the larger population as an original member, an Original Original, and the story of the formless would be added to our records and the history lessons in our schools.

"I think we should talk to Jason about how to engage the formless," I said. "For the future. Should it be necessary."

"That's a good idea," Kent said smiling at me. I think he was proud of my thoughtfulness.

"That can be your project, young Illmatic," Eartha said.

Just as we made our decision, we heard the splash of water and gasping. Delta's fins turned to legs and he climbed out of the fish tank. "What's goin' on around here," he said, now fully clothed and dripping in water. He shook the water out of his hair. The Neo Astronauts sat stunned.
"Who wants to start?" I asked. Eartha, I believe, cut her eyes.

***

Shortly after the meeting I met with Eartha. We hadn't settled matters about the Martian waters, and despite the impact of the discoveries, I really wanted to get back and explore them. Personally, I believed we
needed to map out the waters. How many planets did it interconnect? What was the outcome? But Eartha was firmly against anymore investigations.

"There will be no more inquiries into Mars and its waters," she said.

"With all due respect...

"With all due respect, what?" Eartha asked.

"I believe you sent me on an assignment, and I would like to complete it."

"That assignment is over. I'll have another one to you later in the week."

"I think a decision like this needs a council vote. You aren't in a position to make it alone," I said. Eartha glared at me. I irritated Eartha. I don't know which was more bothersome, my questions or my role in her son's life. She was wrestling with our new society, and I was a reminder of all that she'd missed. Either way, in that moment, I realized that Eartha, despite her warm intentions might never truly connect with me. I stood in the gap between the world she knew and the one she was charged to create. I was a reminder of all they'd done right and all that failed. I was a reminder of Moulan more than I was my own father.

She'd spent years trying to return to Planet Hope, I and Delta brought them all back home in a matter of weeks. She didn't like me and there was little I could do about it. "Do what you think is best, Illmatic. You're going to do what you want to do anyway. Just leave my son out of it."

"Delta and I are a team," I added.

"What's wrong with you?" Eartha belted. "You have no boundaries. No sense of fear. No sense of loss. No respect." Eartha said, rubbing her brow. No, it wasn't me she was thinking of. Her mind was elsewhere. We sat in silence as Eartha stared at the rainbow-colored crystals scattered on her desk. Respect? These assumptions about rank and power in our fledgling government weren't sitting well with me. What exactly was it I was supposed to respect? Wasn't respecting life enough?

All of the Neo Astronauts treated me like I was some unruly child, and I was forever in the shadow of their dogma. Maybe this new government wasn't such a good idea. Is this what I fought for? Eartha continued to rub her brow. I would stand here until she found an answer. Finally, she looked at me. "Yes, the waters do need to be investigated. All I ask is that you stay present and come back with something other than fins."

"And I won't take Delta, if he doesn't want to go," I said.

"Thank you," she quipped.

"But I would like to take Jason," I added. I could feel the heat dart from Eartha's temples. But she composed herself before the temperature could shift in the room.

"Lovely," she added. "I'm sure he'll be an asset. Be sure to shut the door behind you." But I wasn't finished, I thought.

"Yes you are," Eartha added. I stepped back being sure to close the narrow fuchsia door as I left.

Chapter 11

Running Deep

JASON was too happy to return to Mars on a mission.

"I get to be an official ambassador," he said sarcastically. I decided to show Jason around Planet Hope. He checked out our architecture, our museums, and such; but he really just wanted to enjoy nature. I took him to the Enchanted Forest.

"I came here a lot as a firefly," he said. "Pretty place." He seemed to have enjoyed his life as a firefly. While I wanted to gain insight into Mars, I also wanted to understand more about this life in the formless and the choices he made for 3D life.

"Which do you like better?" I asked. "Being a firefly or being human?" He thought about it, clasping his hands behind his back and lifting his chin as if he was giving weighty thought to the question.

"They both give you perspective," he said. "I can't say I like one better than the other. Humans, I think, are better storytellers," he said. I couldn't argue that one. I told him about my experience in my other lives, being careful to skirt around details about Carcine and Delta. I did mention that I had bouts with love, which Jason found more fascinating than anything else.

“ Which life did you like better?” he asked.

“I can’t say,” I responded.

“Which guy did you like better?” he asked. “Did it depend on the lifetime?” I didn’t know what to say. “I’m asking too much, aren’t I? Humans make love so multilayered and complicated,” he said. “In the formless, love doesn’t have so many shades. We’re all one.”

“What’s love like as a firefly?” I asked.

“We don’t think about it much,” he said. I laughed.

We walked across the Field of the Yellow Lady and wound up in the spot where Moulan’s virtual world used to be. All that was left were a few gold bricks.

“So this is it, huh?,” Jason said, looking around. “Any water around here?” he asked.

“No,” I said. “The closest lake is on the other side of the planet. Then I recalled the underground maze filling with water. “Wait, there must be water underground.”

“Oh there is,” he said. “The question is where? So much of this world has shifted since I left.” Jason got on his knees and crawled around.

“Jason, did you know Moulan?” I asked.
“No,” he responded, patting around on the ground. “Oh wait, I think she swatted at me once during the firefly days.”

“And before then?” I asked. But Jason was preoccupied with listening for sounds in the terra.

“Jason,” I said. “How can we engage with the formless?” Jason stopped crawling around and sat on his heels.

"What do you mean?" he asked.

"Planet Hope wants to be a balanced society. We want to avoid the mistakes of Earth and respect all life. We're trying. You brought it to our attention that we're ignoring the choice for potentiality in the 3D, and we want to build healthy relationships with your life form."

"But I'm the only one left," Jason reminded me.
I kneeled beside him. "Jason, both you and I know that that's impossible. Potentiality is infinite. They may not be here. They may be in other life forms. It may not be a form you know, but they do exist." Jason looked at me blankly.

"Are you saying you want us to come home, Rayla?" Jason asked, his eyes twinkling. "Do you know what you're asking?"

"So you aren't the last one," I said.

"I'm a survivor Rayla, much like you. But I know the power of adaptation," he said.

Jason and I continued crawling around on the ground listening for water. At one point I just watched as Jason pressed himself against the soil. He lay so still he was nearly camouflaged. Did he learn this in his insect life? Jason intrigued me. He was a walking mystery that I felt compelled to unravel. Here was a man who not only changed form but remembers his existence pre-3D. I had to learn more. Jason turned his head slowly and mashed his other ear to the ground. He pulled back to his knees, whipped out a knife, and stabbed it into the ground. A geyser sprung up. He put his lips to the stream and swallowed hard.

"Well, Rayla. We can navigate the waters from here or we can start on Mars. Which end of infinity would you like to enter first?"

"Mars," I said.

"I think I'm going to like our friendship," Jason retorted. "You should drink," he said, waving his hand towards the geyser as if I needed direction. "It's everything."

Chapter 12

Starman

LUBA begged to come along with Jason and I to Mars. Eartha and the Neo astronauts weren't thrilled about the trip, and they were equally unamused by Luba's accompaniment. "She hasn't been trained," Sui Lee reminded me. "And you don't know her."

"I don't know anybody," I reminded Sui Lee. "This whole experience is new, but I trust Luba." We decided, to simplify matters, that Luba could keep watch in the apartment, while Jason and I navigated. This way, Luba could live the Martian life like she wanted, while Jason and I figured out the path of the waters. Delta decided to skip this trip.

"I can't do this one," Delta said. We were seated on a hill overlooking Obama City just as the sun was setting. The two moons were fading into play. Just a few short moons ago, this land was war-torn. We were stabilized now. We were our only enemy.

Delta was unnerved. He was really wrestling with his Merman transformation. The entire experience was very unsettling for him, and there was nothing I could say to soothe him."I have some explorations of my own," he said. But it wasn't the fear of uncontrollable transformation that irked Delta. He was bothered by the peace. "I've never felt so connected, so at peace in my life as I was in those waters," he added. "It was as if that was the true me."

"Maybe it is," I said.

"There's no reason for me to feel so connected," he said. "None at all."

"Maybe you should talk to Eartha about it," I said. "Do you know how you were born?" I asked.

"Do you?" he said with irritation.

I was treading more uncomfortable waters, but Jason was right. Some of us on Planet Hope had no idea how we were born. We each had one parent. Some of us had two or three.

"Maybe you'll find your answers in the Martian waters," I added, hoping he'd change his mind.

"I need to do something for me this time," Delta said, blowing smoke from his firestick into the wind. I was empathetic to Delta's confusion, but I didn't like the implication that everything else he'd done in the past was about me. Naturally, he read my thoughts.

"Much of my past was about you," he said turning to face me. "I don't have a problem with that. I love you. But there are some things I need to figure out for myself."

"You couldn't figure it out after you abandoned me in the Enchanted Forest with Carcine and went off to protect Moulan?" I asked. "That wasn't enough time?"

Delta sighed. "Apparently, not." It was a low blow, but I was weary of everyone looking to me as some kind of a burden they needed to hand off. "I apologize," I said. Delta didn't respond. "Say something," I insisted, shoving him softly. Delta's annoyance melted. "I hope you get a good workout in those waters. That shove was nothing," he yammered. We watched the sky blacken and the two moons hovered higher.

"With all the power Jason could have in the formless, why take form?" Delta asked, not expecting me to answer. "You take form for a reason, a purpose. You don't just meander about."
"Maybe you do," I said. "How would we know?"

"When I was a Merman, I could feel him as if he were part of the water," Delta said. "But not just him. There was a presence."
"The other formless?" I asked. Delta shrugged. "Who knows." I wanted to press on, but this was our last night together. Delta was trying his best to live in the present, a point of focus I had to respect. I kissed him on the cheek, and we sat in the light of the two moons. Yes, there was beauty in the present.

***

Back on Mars, Jason and I left Luba at the apartment. As expected, she was entranced by the entertaining neighbors and their personal foibles.
"Life," she cooed. I brought Moulan's book with me along with my own and decided to leave both in the apartment. I reminded Luba of their importance.

"I know," she said. "You don't have to explain."

"Where are your friends, Jason" Luba asked. "Will I have to show myself around, too?" Luba's impatience wasn't something I'd planned on.
"I gotta' work on that," Jason said matter-of-factly, as he packed his bag with deep-sea swimming gear.

"Who doesn't have friends?" Luba said, crossing her legs on Jason's giant red couch. But her pouting was eclipsed when a short man with a red fuzzy mustache in a shower above us began singing ancient D'Angelo songs.

"He's delightful," Luba said, completely transfixed.

***

Jason and I flew to the Cove in a small craft. I shielded the craft to neutralize energy fields and ward off detection. We hid the craft in a cave, climbed down the pit swiftly, and prepared to dive. We put our gear on and sat at the edge of the clear water. The enveloping quiet became its own vibration of sound. I thought of the Crystal Cove.
"Do you feel the stillness," Jason asked. I did. "This is what it feels like before form." The crystals embedded in the walls shimmered. "Are you ready?" he asked.

A yellow firefly whizzed by. We both watched it zip into the black of the cave and flicker away.

"Yes," I said. Jason smiled, attached his head gear. I did the same and we both dove in.

Underwater life is eerie. Maybe I was just used to navigating the skies stars or running along the terrestrial, but this life underwater took some getting used to. The trees and branches webbed like spindly ghosts of a land unknown. Our swimming gear enabled us to speak and motion easily, which helped, but this water space was not my world. No amount of well-intentioned technology could ease my discomfort below sea level. Technically, I could have surrounded us by a force field, which could have kept the waters from touching our skin and encapsulating oxygen, but these technofiber bodysuits that we wore made that unnecessary. How many of my other powers were unnecessary in water space? Now probably wasn't the time to think about it.

I felt like an imposter in these magical waters. The sea life sensed it, too. Their foreboding eyes wide with curiosity, the slivering fish scaled by us like we were invisible. We swam for some time. With every kick I felt fear mounting. Why was I afraid? I'd circled time and back and never did I feel this uncomfortable. The waters grew darker. We passed an array of sizable rainbow-colored fish and hulking mammals, all two to three times our size. There was no sign of a glowing Sphinx anywhere. I wanted to leave.

"Wasn't it this way?" I asked through my mask, pointing toward a series of pits. Was I about to hyperventilate? I steadied my breath.

Jason didn't seem to notice.

"I think so," said Jason. But he didn't sound so sure. "It didn't take this long to transform last time," he whispered.

Jason and I swam deeper and deeper. There was more water above us than below. The thought of it made me feel like sinking, but I flutter-kicked on. Like a comet streaking the sky, a small black image whizzed by so fast, the rush of it pushed us back.

We scurried behind a bed of rocks and watched as this submarine of sorts landed at the bottom of the ocean. Three shadowy figures in all black slipped out of the submarine, swam upwards of the floor and formed a diamond. The diamond spun and increased in speed, propelling a rush of bubbles and force. Jason and I grabbed on to the rocks to keep from blowing away. I closed my eyes in fear but forced myself to reopen them. With each rotation, the propellers' figures dissipated, breaking into tiny black shells and stacking on top of one another until two giant faces formed into a mask with a splash of blue down the forehead of one and pink on the other. The lips of both masks moved in harmony.

"Welcome," they said in a high-tinged voice that rang like a song.

"We're looking for the Sphinx," I said. "We're looking for Moulan."

The black shells of the mask reconfigured and aligned into the shape of a narrow tunnel. I motioned for Jason to follow me as I swam through the entrance. With each kick, my legs went numb until both moved in a seamless motion. My legs were now fins, my black suit had vanished, and an ivy-colored moss adorned my bosom. Jason was now a Merman, too. When we exited the coral tunnel, the glow of the green Sphinx greeted us.

"You've returned," I could hear Moulan singing. "And you've brought a friend. A new one."

We swam through the parted mouth of the Sphinx and were in a new world of underwater wonder. Whereas Planet Hope was littered with crystals, this world was sprinkled with pink and silver shells. Sea dwellings of pastel shells and bright coral were the vestiges of sunlight in this blue aqua world. Stunning Mermen and Mermaids swam with their heads tilted high, an ode to their own regality and striking beauty. They didn't notice Jason and I at all. And their bodies moved as fluidly as the waves they swam under. One Mermaid with short black hair wore smudges of sparking blue on her lips, which matched her blue tail. She snaked into an eight before flicking her tail in our face and dashing off. A silver gate lay several meters before us and floated open as we approached, revealing none other than Moulan, seated side saddle in all her glory on the back of a giant black seahorse. Her minty green tail flipped a bit—a move that matched the twirl of her pearl- laced wrist. Her once dark locks, now sea green sparkles, were bundled high on her head. Ropes of fist-sized pearls hung so low from her neck that it covered her bosom.

Her sparkly mint cape flapped with the flow of the water. It was big enough to blanket us all. I smiled to myself. I missed this woman. I missed this mysterious mother of mine, who pushed me beyond every realm of reality I'd ever known. I was being pushed again, even now, as we looked into one another's dark eyes, seeing ourselves in one another; seeing our potential and our enemy all in the same gaze. Maybe I should hug her, I thought. But Moulan wasn't one for cuddling, and she cut the temptation with a curt smile.

"Nice, isn't it?" she said, tilting her head ever so slightly. "It takes some getting used to, but it's rather cozy. Much like a never-ending warm bubble bath or a steamy hot shower after a long, arduous ax fight. Who's your friend?"

"Jason. He's one of the original members of Planet Hope—an Original Original."

Moulan shrugged a tiny shoulder and circled Jason on her sea horse, her cape flapping in the wave. She looked him up and down with an eye of intrigue, but Jason was unfazed.

"You took form?" she said.

"Makes it easier to navigate," Jason whiffed.

Moulan grunted and treaded off. Her cape billowed around her as she swiveled to face us.

"So they're too afraid to take to the waters, and they sent you two down to find me. How. Unwittingly. Predictable," she sighed. "Tell your friends, and I repeat your friends, on dear Planet Hope that I am quite happy where I am. They don't have to worry about any interference in their pathetic unfettered mediocre affairs by the likes of me," Moulan spat.

"We just want to know what all is down here," I said.

"Where is Delta?" she cooed.

"He chose not to come," I said.

"Too embarrassed to face me, can admire that," Moulan said. "Give him my love." Should I tell her about Delta's Merman moments? She probably already knew.

"Gorgeous, aren't they?" she remarked, pointing to the men and women swimming outside her chambers. A bevy of curvaceous women with hair ensnared in the waters and chiseled men all with fins moved by. They were a sight to behold, but they trailed around with about as much life as a doorknob. Who were these people? Where did they come from?

"How many planets do these waters interconnect with?" I asked.

"Questions. Questions and more questions. Really, Rayla can you ever just enjoy the magic of the moment," Moulan asked. "It's a wonder that you're even able to survive this, better yet be amongst it.

People all across the universe have marveled at the wonder of the Mermaid and Merman. They've questioned their existence for an eternity. Half human, half sea animal. You have the privilege to be amongst them, to be one of them. Appreciate the moment. Look at that one," Moulan said, pointing to a Mermaid with red curls and a silver star painted on her cheek. "She has freckles."
But this mystery water made me feel much like Delta did on the Martian terrain. Yes, the waves were hypnotic, but this was not a place to relax. It felt like I was in some sort of past.

"This is a site to behold," Jason said, mesmerized by the sea people swimming by. "This life is so ancient."

"See, someone has an appreciation for life," Moulan said, spitting out the word 'life' like a dagger. "Antiquity has many wonders," Moulan purred. Jason was lost in wonderment.

"Moulan, please just answer the question," I asked. Moulan shook her head in annoyance.

"All of them," she retorted. "The waters connect all the planets in the universe. Don't tell me they want you to map it out. You'll have to move down here for three lifetimes or so to figure it out."

"Who uses these waterways?" I asked.

"The sea animals and us. Who else would be down here? You know I have a penchant for safeguarding the treasured things in the universe, and I felt this waterway needed some relative protection since none of you other than your new pal here seems to know or care that it exists. Your friends are careless. You can thank me later."

Moulan rose from her sea horse and flitted to a floating mirror. She adjusted her tresses, pulled out a match of green color from her bosom, and painted it on her lips.

"You couldn't master the Akashic records so you became the gatekeeper to these waterway portals?"

"One day, you're going to understand my value, missy. But as always, it will be too late. Too late, too late, too late," she repeated. Moulan looked at me as if for the first time. She was staring at my mouth.

"You need color on your lips. Follow me." I swam off with Moulan into more private chambers.

***

Moulan's private Coral Reef was water-free. As soon as we entered, our legs returned, and Moulan was back to adorning her green, long and lace frocks. She'd assembled a makeshift underwater cottage with a tea room mildly similar to the last, but it felt off. This cottage was lonely and I found myself feeling sorry for Moulan, my mother under the sea. Was she destined to be in these private safeguards forever? Did she have any friends? Moulan dragged a heavy silver treasure chest across the floor, flipped the lock open, dug in, and pulled out a tube of red color. She mashed it on my lips.

"I'm glad you're here," Moulan said. "You look good with fins. Color on your lips brings out the shimmer in your scales." Her insistence on glamour was always comical to me, but I'd come to appreciate it. She gave me a lookover. I guess she approved. I suppose this is what mothers do.

"You didn't read my book did you?" she asked, putting a teaspoon of moss in a tea kettle.

"No," I said. "Not yet." But I did bring it with me. Moulan seemed disappointed. So I told her about the demands of world building and my trip to Mars, hoping to explain away my busyness.

"Why haven't you done any more soul journeys?" she asked, pouring the green liquid in two large sea shells. She handed one to me. "I didn't have a reason to. We've found the Neo Astronauts." Moulan took a sip from her shell.

"Rayla, you've learned to do something that most people can't. You need to use your ability as a resource. They may not value it in this new Planet Hope you're building, but you must."

"I need to be present," I said.

"Present?" Moulan said, raising her eyebrow. "And what is that?" she asked, floating off. Moulan pulled out a bottle from the cupboard; she poured a steamy liquid into two tea cups. She sent one my way, using her mind of course, and I caught it at the handle. I took a sip.

"Why are we drinking out of so many different vessels?" I asked.

"I don't want to save them for a rainy day," she miffed.

"Are you going to tell me how I was born?" I asked.

"I don't see how that's relevant."

"Neither does my father," I added.

Moulan twisted her flush lip. She was thinking of my father, but I couldn't read her. I never could. "I could say you were born in a manger, but I don't see what difference it makes. As you've discovered, you've always been here in one shape, form, fashion, or another. It doesn't matter how you came into this one."

"You say that because you know how I was born and I don't," I added.

Moulan wasn't as biting as she'd been in the past. We weren't fighting. I had no need to raise my sword. It's as if she'd been defeated. Was she happy here? But Moulan is never one to lick her wounds, and I'd be a fool to think she was ever in a position of limited advantage.

"I'm fine, Rayla," she said, reading my mind. "I like this sea just fine," she said, returning to a mirror that adorned her wall.

"You are right. This waterway does have countless portals and dimensions. The sea is deep. It's a repository for many things. Whereas the books were holders of lifetimes, this sea seems to be a bedrock of collective memories, emotions, some of which take form. I've tried cataloging it all, but I've learned that such things are pointless. Any unacknowledged emotion seems to connect with others of like mind and emerge into a form."

"What form?" I asked.

"Mermaids, honey. Look around you?," she said. "These Mermaids spring up out of a collective set of human emotions. There's a new one all the time. It's rather hard to manage. These fish people are a walking poem. When they've moved on from the emotion, they swim up one of these portals, walk onto shore, and live a new life. It's a cathartic process, I suppose."
"And some come down here to just escape it all. Like your other friend." I bit my lip.

"There's nothing down here for you, Rayla. No wars, no battles. No love," she added. "You'll have to find that elsewhere."

"You're down here," I said.

"For now," she added. Was Moulan escaping from her trials like Carcine? Was Moulan a manifestation of a bundle of emotions that needed to be released? Was she in a state of remorse? Was she looking to one day emerge on white sands anew? Could I help?

I looked to the trail of floating sea people. "They're like ghosts of the waters," I said.

"Do I look like a ghost?" Moulan snapped. Moulan walked out of her fortress, and I followed. She didn't want my pity. Back in the waters, our fins returned.

"Looking for something to do?" she said angrily. Moulan was livid. Was sympathy really that bad? "There is a waterway that goes from here to Planet Hope," she said speedily. She zipped about and I had to hustle to keep up with her. "There's a lot of traffic going in and out of it. I don't really know what that's about."

"What do you mean, traffic?" I said.

"There's a lot of people becoming Mermaids coming out of Planet Hope. A pipeline coming right out of Shogun City and then going up another waterway that goes to Earth. You want a task? You looking to save the planet? You're bored by your procedural duties that daddy gave you? Well there's a mystery for you.

"Are they building something?" I asked.

"I. Don't. Know. I stay clear of Planet Hope. And Planet Hope better stay clear of me." Moulan spun into a bevy of figure eights, stopped in my face and swam off.

Chapter 13

Silver Slippers or Ruby Ones?

I returned to the silver gateway where I met Moulan and looked around for Jason. Moulan was poised coolly on her black sea horse. "Do you know where Jason is?" I asked. A black-tailed Mermaid, all sashay and swish, swam by. Her dark ponytail hit my face.

"He's decided to stay," the black-tailed one said, eyeing me like a hungry one does a meal. Her dark eyes could swallow us all whole. Looking at her was like taking in my reflection, but we didn't look alike. Something about the fluid swish in her waist made me feel childlike, naïve, inexperienced. But I didn't look away and the black-tailed one smiled.

"Rayla, meet Eleven Brown," Moulan said. "She's a sister to you. Probably the only sister you'll ever have."

"How are we sisters?" I asked.

"Because I said you are," Moulan said curtly.

"Hello, sister," Eleven said, slinking around me. She was the only Mermaid I witnessed whose scales and adornments were all black. "You're quite impressive. Maybe one day someone will write my story, too," she said.

"I'm going to need to speak to Jason myself," I said.
"You don't trust me?" Eleven asked, circling me. She swam above my head and dropped her ponytail in my face. I pushed it away.

"I'm staying," Jason said, appearing out of a hail of bubbles. "I don't know what came over me, but I feel this is where I need to be," he said. "It's an ancient world. It's like the beginning."

"A beginning," Moulan echoed. Moulan kept her back to me.

"Yes, a beginning. We like beginnings," Eleven said.

"I understand. But we do have a mission, Jason," I reminded him. I was getting Carcine flashbacks. No, he was not staying and nothing could convince me that Moulan or Eleven, for that matter, weren't putting Jason in a trance. A wave of bubbles flooded my face, and when they cleared, Jason was nearly a 100 meters away. I swam off to catch him, moving at a speed I'd never known. Where was he going?

Jason dipped through dips and caverns, as if he's lived here his whole life. I was gaining on him, but each time I got within reach, he'd flick his tail and a tidal wave of bubbles would whip me back. He did this six or seven times. The last time, I emerged in a cavalcade of sharks. All nine of them were after me. I dipped through a cove, swam out of the other side, and the sharks were waiting for me. I blasted through, circled around, and spotted Jason nearing the surface. I narrowed my gaze and pushed harder, faster. Sunlight was pouring into the waters. I was on his tail when, suddenly, he nose-dived into a dark cave below. Where was he going?

I followed but the cave was too dark to decipher anything. I navigated through and came up through the other end. The water was cooler. I looked about and didn't see him at all. The water was more shallow here. I could see the bottom and the surface in one. Did he go above ground? I swam to the surface and my fins turned to legs, I fell a bit and had to use the power of my arms to lift up. I made it to the surface, gasping for breath.

"There she is," someone yelled. I was yanked out of the water. The sun stung my eyes. My eyes were burning. My vision was blurry. Someone was holding me. Delta Blue looked into my eyes. "Thought we'd lost you for a second," he said. Delta held me close. We were in a small boat. A small city lined the sands a few miles away. Delta kissed my cheek. The sun was high in the sky. It's high noon. The town was unfamiliar. I held Delta close but my eyes were scanning the perimeter. Where was I?

Chapter 14

Really Love

DELTA was steering the boat, his hands clasped the thick wheel. He looked very much like a sea captain. I guess he was a sea captain. He was sporting all white. A white hat with a brim, a white shirt with white buttons, and white pants. The boat rocked and the glass of water on the deck fell over and rolled to the boat's corner. It was a boat for living. There were cots below, closets, food. I sat on a bench in some sort of red swimwear that didn't cover my legs. A navy blue towel was wrapped around me.

"That fall musta' got to ya," he said. "You seem like you're shaken up a bit." There was no shore as far as the eye could see at this point. But it was clear that this was not Planet Hope, and Delta wasn't Delta or at least not the Delta I know. Who was I?

"Where are we?" I asked. "We're about halfway between The Canary Islands and Monte Carlo," Delta said, keeping his eye on the path ahead. "Don't worry," there's no storm coming. The place where we're staying is private, so you won't have to worry about anyone hassling you. Perfect place for a honeymoon."

I looked at my left hand. I was wearing a ring with a silver rock. Usually in my soul journeys, I would go into a previous lifetime with no consciousness of my present life. I would arrive completely connected to my past life, its world and nuances, it's color and flavor. But here I was completely aware of who I was. I was Rayla of Planet Hope, and I was totally disconnected from this water, this boat, and my whereabouts. This was not a soul journey. This was not a past life.

"What year is this?" I asked Delta.

"Whoa? Did you hit your head down there, too? My goodness. It's 1958. Don't worry. We'll be to shore in no time. Just rest awhile. We've got a lot of money to win." Money?

When Delta fell asleep, I dug in his pocket looking for identification. His boaters' license said that his name was Winn Kincot. He was an American ex pat and U.S. soldier living in Nice, France. Okay. So I'm on Earth. But who was I? I ransacked the quarters looking for a hint of anything. I found a name stitched in a woman's red leather handbag. The bag had a 45 pistol and a passport. The passport read Numidya Manad of Morocco. My picture, a black and white image with my hair pulled back. was plastered on the side.

Numidya?

***

We got to shore before sundown. Delta knew this town. The buildings were no more than two floors. The streets were narrow. I wore a pink skirt and a scarf hung over my head. Our arms were linked and passersby smiled at the sight of us. The street was a market. Smells of spices and car exhaust infused the air. Music spilled out of cars and restaurants. A few people pulled four-legged cattle on a leash. We stopped at a building that looked identical to the others. Delta said we were staying at an inn, and he paid a tall man with a pointy beard behind a desk a stack of colored paper so that we could stay in a square room.

"The tournament is tomorrow," he added once we'd settled in. "You wanna' rest or you want to hit the streets?"

“Rest. Please, let’s rest.” I sat in the narrow bed and urged Delta to lie beside me. The room had one window that faced the street, and the night noise of happy people rose with ease past our window and beyond.

“Tell me more,” I said, “about this tournament.”

“I should be asking you,” he added. “You’re the master of the game.”

“What game?” I asked. Delta turned to me puzzled. I tried to play it all off.

“I just love the way you explain it,” I cooed. He called the game poker. It was a card game, much like the ones the Neo Astronauts played the night we were in Moulan’s place and Lagos launched the takeover. Delta explained the rules, he talked about signals and cues and how we would win. At the conclusion of the game, we would leave for France and ‘live our life on the seas.’ Delta seemed to feel that our future would be dictated by this game of painted paper.

“Then let’s practice,” I said. Delta smiled.

***

The innkeeper led us to a back room. The room was choking in smoke. Several men were seated and bent over a table. A few women sauntered about. Chips were stacked. The inn keeper ushered us inside. We joined the table. A man in a bow tie handed us cards. It was a game of finding pairs. The game was rather simple, but the men seemed to study their cards carefully, mulling over decisions. I didn’t understand their hesitancy. And as I stacked deck after deck, and my colored chips piled up, the men grew more tense.

“Who are you, woman?” one man asked. He unbuttoned the top button of his white shirt and tipped his hat lower.

"Numidya," I said.

"Anyone with a name like that means business," another one joked. I guess I was winning. At the end of the game, the colored chips were exchanged for colored paper and Delta was ecstatic.

"You do it every time," he said. "Unbelievable." Delta wanted to head back to bed, but I told him I needed air.

"You should walk these streets alone," he said. I had to remind myself that this was not the Delta of Planet Hope. No one ever questioned my fighting skills.

Outside, I leaned against the cool inn wall and looked to the moon. I would never get over Earth's single ball of a moon. The streets had quieted some, but my mind was racing. Do I go back to the water and seek the Sphinx? Do I teleport back to Planet Hope? Both were perfectly logical options but neither felt right. Where was Jason? Did it matter? How did I wind up in this world fully conscious as Rayla? Who was Numidya?

A figure whirled out of the shadows and reached for my necklace. I knocked him to the wall. Another grabbed me around my waist, trying to carry me off.

"We don't lose to women," he muttered in my ear. I flipped him over, grabbed the knife from his waist band, and stabbed the two men running up behind me. I stomped the one on the floor in the neck, smashed the heads of the two who'd been wounded together, and they crashed to the floor. They were all rolling in pain, I pulled back to land a heavier blow when a crème colored car with no top flashed its lights and pulled up. The hat was low, but I'd recognize that voice anywhere. "Get in, Illmatic." The man tipped his hat up enough for his profile to emerge from the shadow. "Carcine?"

Chapter 15

She's Always in My Hair

CARCINE was cruising the streets like we had all the time in the world. The stars dotted the sky, and Carcine kept one hand on the wheel and tossed a white dress in my lap with the other.

"You've got blood on you," he said. "That's not a good look here." I slipped out of one old world outfit and put on another. There were shoes with little heels on the floor. Carcine pulled up to a small beach, stepped out, grabbed my bloody clothes, tossed them on a few logs, and lit a match. I left my shoes in the car and hopped out after him. The fire crackled and I watched the ashes float in the air.

"You can't go back into the water 'til the new tide comes in," Carcine said. "That's the way it works on this side. All Mermaids on this side of things reenter with the tide. That gives you three days."

"Three days. I've heard that before," I said. Carcine ignored my sarcasm.

"Monte Carlo is the gambling capitol of the world. The best of the best come here for fortune, fame, and notoriety. And after your stunt back there, you're on the fast track to the latter."

"Why are you here?" I asked. He didn't answer me.

"Your name is Numidya. You were born in the Atlas Mountains and made your way to the city hustling on the street for money. One day, some men left you for dead, you rolled into the sea. The water gave you life. You survived as a Mermaid, and every season you return for money and vengeance. Delta, or whatever he's calling himself these days, waits for you every summer. He burns an altar of sea shells, oregano, and lime to you. You come to him, you make him money. You celebrate your love, and you go below until the next solstice."

"My name is Rayla," I told him.

"Well in this one you're Numidya," he said. "People hope to see you every solstice because you grant wishes."

"Carcine, in my soul journeys I never retained my Rayla memory consciously," I said.

"You're not in the stream of lifetimes; you're in the ocean of myths."

"And what does that mean?" I asked.

"It means you play out the script as given, you inspire the world, and you go back to wherever you came from."

"The sea?" I asked him.

"They think you come from the sea. We know you're from Planet Hope. But whether it's a planet they've never heard of or a sea they'll never know at the end of the day it's all one big myth."

"I won't accept that," I said. "Who is Numidya?"

"She's a story," he said. "Whether it's you as Numidya or somebody else, there is always a Numidya. You just happened to come out of the sea at the right time. I guess your energy matched her mythical one and, voila, here you are. Don't blame me, you called it." I watched as the last of my old world dress disintegrated. Carcine stomped out the fire with his heavy black shoe. " Hungry?" he asked.

***

A round woman with a red scarf and crème kaftan served food to us. We were in another room in the back of a dwelling. The small room was lit with candles. The food—a yellow rice, carrots, tomatoes, and peppers—was swimming in a red sauce. The woman smiled at us and left us alone. Carcine grabbed a spice shaker and dabbed.

"I guess I use this out of habit. Khalilah always seasons to perfection," he said.

"So you're a Merman now?" I asked.

"I grant wishes and go back below the sea just as you do or will do. It's a good way to keep the spirits up. And it's a little easier to manage than leading a rebel crew of high-strung warriors or owning a nightclub that doubles as an astronaut hub," he said. "Besides," he said. "I'm granting your wish," he added.

"My wish for what?" I said.

"To go on a date," he added, tucking a cloth at his neck to protect himself from the platter of food. "In our life of war, we never went on a date."

I wanted to smatter Carcine with sarcasm, but it seemed callous at this point. I responded with words he didn't expect. I thanked him. "Wishes don't always come when you ask, but they're always right on time," he added. I laughed. Carcine told stories of other wishes he'd granted. He won money for a young boy who needed medicine for his mother, he helped a lost woman find her way home. He even found a soul mate for an old man who'd lost his boyfriend at sea. This wish granting was a nice juxtaposition to living in the sea.

"Sea life can get a little boring," he said. "But I welcome boredom after what we'd been through. I needed a break."

I shared with him Moulan's summation of the sea and how it houses emotions. "Works for me," Carcine said. "I don't talk to her much, but I don't need to either." It was nice chatting with Carcine. My anger aside, it was his friendship that I missed most. It was nice to speak freely, moving beyond our tenuous past and arriving at some sense of peace with one another. While our friendship remained, it was clear to both of us that we would never be together in the way we'd once dreamed. I'd decided to stop analyzing him not so long ago. I'd decided to stop assessing the how's and why's. I would never understand his motivations and he likely didn't know them enough to explain them to me. But I did have one question.

"Carcine, will you ever come back to Planet Hope?" Carcine's eyes didn't flicker. He munched on his carrots, giving a silence that inferred contemplation. But Carcine was a man who'd dumped his worries and what ifs in the sea some time ago. Bliss was his state, for now.

"If there's a need for me, I'll consider it," he said. "If you want me to come back, I will," he added. "But I know that need isn't compelling."

"Your ultimate decision won't have anything to do with me," I said. Carcine tilted his head slightly. A ripple ran across his forehead and disappeared. He' d tossed whatever thought he'd had to the ocean of the past.

"Do you like this place?" he asked. I looked about. The dwelling had a charm that I accredit to the sensation of the food and candlelight.

"Yes, yes I do."

"Good," he said. "Now my wish has been granted." I didn't want to reveal my smile, but I couldn't help it.

***

Carcine dropped me off at the inn. I could still hear the waves on the ocean kiss the shore.

"Three days, Rayla," Carcine said, as I opened the door. He looked at me plainly and simply. The moonlight hit his face. His square jaw and heavy eyes were calling to me. "You have three days 'til the New Moon comes in. That first night of the new moon you make it into the waters before sunrise."

"And if I don't?" I asked.

"Then you have to wait 'til the full moon," he says. "But if you miss a full moon cycle, you're stuck here. Got it?" I heard everything Carcine said, but my mind was racing to find the logic. Why one moon cycle? Why not two or three? Why not a season? Who came up with this rule?

"You know what, don't worry about it. I'll come find you. I see how this is going," he said. Carcine kissed me on the cheek. I slipped out of the car and he raced off.

Chapter 16

More Today Than Yesterday

I didn't sleep long. Delta was up bright and early. His giddiness was unsettling and incredibly impractical. But I reminded myself that this new Delta or Winn, was not someone I truly knew. I would need to be easy and be patient with him, this stranger who appeared to be Delta in this alternate space on the other side of the Ocean of Myths. Delta drew the curtains and stood in the gaze of the rising sun. I yearned to sleep the day away; but this was the first of three big days, according to Delta, and his future was resting on my winner's aptitude. I wanted the sunlight out of my face. I no longer wanted to be here. My patience had worn thin already and I wasn't even out of the bed.

Three days.

"I was hoping," Delta said, sitting beside me with a plate of food in his hand, "that this time you would stay," he said. Stay? Delta stuck a forkful of egg whites in my mouth.

"Stay," I added. "I can't do that." I tried to say it with the pleasantness of a fantastic water nymph. But I was hot at the very thought of it.

"I know," Delta continued sticking a mouthful of juicy coconut

in my mouth. "But I've fallen in love with you, and each year when you return to the sea my heart is ripped in two. I don't think I can take it anymore."
Delta's haunting brown eyes were lost in love, and my temperament couldn't absorb the sorrow he tried to convey. I didn't share his sentiment, obviously. To embrace the myth was to embrace a lie. Should I tell him my story? This Delta would never understand. Truth would destroy him; fantasy gives him life; and to embrace the myth and this girl coyness was my protection in this unfamiliar world of sand, oceans, and people and gamers. Where was Jason, I wondered.

"Is there another?" Delta asked, his eyes pleading. Did he sense my wondering thoughts? I couldn't underestimate this Delta nor his desire. He tried to put another forkful of coconut in my mouth but I pushed it away, slipped out of the bed and looked to the sea. Delta eased behind me, ensnaring me in his embrace. I wanted him to go away. I hated not being able to say so.

"I can provide a beautiful life for you beyond the sea," he whispered. "I can provide anything you need."

I slipped out of Delta's grasp. I wasn't interested in pretending, nor did I want to master the finesse of guile and deception that women in this world used as their primary defense. Could I teleport from here? I searched the room, looking through drawers, patting walls. Was there an escape hatch? Was there another connection to Planet Hope besides sailing through the underworld of the sea? I felt trapped and I didn't like it. Delta watched me totally puzzled. There was a knock at the door. "Our ride is here," Delta said.

***

The casino was a castle in the bright sun. The sun was so magnificent in this world it was nearly indecipherable from the sparkling granules of yellow. This world was whitewashed in illumination. Delta, still in his all white wear ushered me inside and I, as his Mermaid on land wore all white with a flair of a fin at the ankles. All the opulence of Alhambra punctuated the sea salt that hung in the air. The blood red velvet curtains flanked the hall, meeting the garnet colored rugs like a sea ebbing the shore. The jewel colored tapestries hung from sky high ceilings and tower sized columns pushed the ceiling to the horizon. But neither the dark rainbow of precious stones nor the twinkling walk ways could mask that this was a world where danger lurked in the friendliest of smiles. Everyone in this room wore black. Everyone in this room wore a grin that didn't gleam. Was Jason among them?' I wondered. But Jason's hypnotism in the waters affirmed for me that this was not his world. Despite myself, I decided to look for him anyway.

"Excuse me," I told Delta, and moved between the slinking people in black. I darted through crowds and tables, doing quick studies of faces. These faces were familiar. I felt that I'd seen some of them before.

"Perhaps they just remind you of someone," a woman's voice whispered in my ear. The voice was much like my own. The black veil cloaked a face that was my own as well.

"You?" I said. You, my double from Shogun City, was hiding out here in this Hall of Games. My stomach turned and the rush of confusion that complicated my relationship to Shogun City made my tongue go dry.

"Yes," she repeated. "You didn't expect me to stay trapped in that greenhouse in Shogun City forever, did you? And you didn't come to check on me," she said, pouting like a child.

"Or me," said the Other Delta. The Delta double of Shogun City accompanied her. He, too, wore the color of the others, adorning a black turban and matching veil. Goodness, how many Deltas were there in this multiverse? How many me's were there?

Yes, I hadn't returned to Shogun City since the new government was formed. I did not check on my or Delta's double. I left that work, and the proposed work of dismantling the doubles to someone else. I wasn't for their abandonment, but Planet Hope had a rule: no artificial intelligence. When Moulan created doubles of the planet's population in an attempt to protect the people from their own reality, she'd broken that rule. The new council's only resolution was to have them taken apart. My arguments protecting AI life fell flat.

"I apologize," I said.

"They wanted to dismantle us. But you knew that," You said.

"And you did nothing," the Other Delta muttered.

"As usual," You remarked.
"I…" but You interrupted me.

"You did nothing," she snapped, wrinkling her nose with distaste. She took a breath, smiled a lethal grin, and continued. "But that's okay," she whined. "We've found life elsewhere."

"First the sea," said the Other Delta.

"And now here," she continued. She leaned into my ear. I stood still just to placate her.

"And you didn't get our permission," You said.

"I can leave," I said. "What's the quickest way out of here?" I asked. "Is it the sea?"

"I don't know if you're welcome in the sea, either," a woman's voice snapped. The hairs on my neck stiffened. Eleven Brown was in the room, and she'd spoken. Eleven's black dress was the essence of seduction. The dress hugged her curves and feathered into a Mermaid's tale. She glided much like a woman in flight, but she was slinking on heels as narrow and tall as the grass in the Field of the Yellow Lady. Her flash of teeth was pleasant and sinister. I wished she'd worn a frown instead. Eleven circled me, eyeing me with a desire I didn't understand.

"I can see why she likes you so much," said Eleven. "You are," she said, pausing to find the word, "intriguing. Are those mysterious eyes really a window to your soul?" she said looking into my eyes before taking a breath. I felt she could suck in my breath and I'd dissipate. I stepped back.

"I don't want to be here anymore than you want me to be," I said.

"Oh, I want you to be here," Eleven said. "I just can't have you living my myth. I'm Numidiya. Winn is mine and this is my world," she said, swirling her hand like a wand. "All the doubles have found this place to be a nice, safe haven for our myriad of interests," she continued.

I looked about. Is this why so many of the faces were familiar? These were the doubles of Planet Hope.

"Not all of them," Eleven continued, reading my mind. I tried to build a forcefield around myself to prevent Eleven from reading more, but the density in this world made it more difficult.

"Don't bother trying to block me," Eleven continued. "I know you better than you know yourself. As does You," she added. "We've become best buds. She's so," she said, curling her eyes again for a hunt for words, "knowledgeable." Where did Eleven come from? Who was she really?

"It doesn't matter where I'm from," Eleven continued.

"What do you want?" I asked.

"What do I want?" she asked, chuckling as if it were funny. "You ask it as if you could give it to me. You must really think you're the one who grants wishes around here," she beamed.

"I'll leave," I said, turning away, but Eleven circled me so fast she was in my face the moment I shifted. Why was I here, I wondered. "Not so fast," Eleven cooed. "Planet Hope must be a lovely world. You're so eager to get back there."

"So you haven't been," I said matter-of-factly. Eleven flashed a half smile. So she wants to go to Planet Hope, but something is preventing her from going. Good to know. And based on the glint in her eye, it seemed as if my force field was working. She couldn't read me anymore.

"We'll play a game," she said. n"If you win, you get to go home. If I win, I get to go to your home and you're welcome to stay here—forever." She wants a swap, but why? Game time was over. I pushed past Eleven and moved into the crowd. I slipped through the web of people in black, some in backless gowns, others in kaftans, most with triangles around their necks. Delta, the Winn Delta, rose from a seat at a game table. "Ready," he said eagerly. A chair beside him awaited me.

"Of course she's ready," Eleven stated. She was seated at the card table, shuffling as she stared my way. Was she a shapeshifter? Was she a person who could vanish and reappear? How did she move so quickly? Eleven sat calmly as if she'd been sitting there all along. You and the Other Delta stood behind her staring me down briefly before moving on. Delta swept his arm as if to usher me to the table. I didn't move.

"We should leave," I told him. "But we just arrived," Delta said, concerned. He looked from me to Eleven. "Give us just a sec," Delta said to Eleven, joining me at my side. "And now he doesn't recognize me," she chirped. "It's your fault," she snipped. "My time is now," Eleven said. The sharpness of her tone rendered Delta frozen. "One million dollars to you, Numidya, if you win. Take it or leave it."

"And if I lose?" I said. "You can work here and pay it off," she said, her cheeks rounding with sarcasm.I turned and headed for the exit. Delta was on my heels. "But Numidya," he called. "As I neared the looming doors of this Hall of Games, they shut. I could feel the eyes of the people in black upon me. I turned once again and Eleven was gliding my way."Welcome to the Hall of Games, Rayla. Play or be played." She continued to walk towards me. Her stealth eyes were fixated on mine."This hall is teleport-proof. So don't try it," she said before flashing the scariest grin of them all."

THE HALL OF GAMES

6

Chapter 17

While My Guitar Gently Weeps

Rules
Rule # 1 Play or be played
Rule #2 Be played or play
Rule #3 Wear dark, dark black
Rule #4 No teleporting
Rule #5 No feathers
Rule #6 No napkin rings

ELEVEN stood at the end of the mirrored hallway twiddling my blood-red feather in her hand. This was not the hallway of my dreams that led to the Crystal Cove. Or was it?

"I can't get it to work," Eleven said, slipping the elegant feather through her slim fingers.

Although I was struck with fear a moment earlier, something about the dimensions of this hallway rang with familiarity. Was the Crystal Cove on the other side of these mirrors?

I'd had enough of these games. I ran full speed towards Eleven, and she ran full speed towards me; and just when I was within reach of her, she ran through me to the other side. What? I pivoted. Eleven stood with a smug look on her face. I ran full speed after her, but this time she ran from me. Again, I pulled hard, was within reach of her, and Eleven pushed a massive door open that led to the outer rims of the galaxy. I stopped at what appeared to be the edge of the universe, the blackness and streaking comets just outside the doorway, but Eleven hovered like a star herself in space.

"Ha," she laughed. "You afraid to come out here with me?" I pulled the door shut, turned about, and Eleven was in my face. Again, I felt like her eyes were sucking me in, but she stepped backwards into the mirror and stood as a reflection. Who was this lady?

"Try it," she said. "You can trust me." She gave an exaggerated doe-eyed blink then stepped out of the reflection. We stood face to face. I wasn't frightened. I wasn't anything.

She circled me. Her gaze penetrated my skin; and when she curved behind me, I shifted, swung my fist, and knocked her to the ground. Eleven clutched her face, screaming. Then she stopped and laughed. There were no cuts, no bruises, just more Eleven smiles. She cocked her head, sat on her bottom, and leaned back onto her forearms.

"You're spunky and not as predictable as I thought," she said. She extended her hand, waiting for me to pull her up. When I didn't, she snickered and, again, pushed herself off the floor. She slid past me. I snatched the feather from her fingertips; and with one flick of the wrist, the feather was an elongated sword. Eleven snatched off her giant black earrings, and each exploded into a 9-inch knife. We were matched in Tiger stance.

I swung with all my might. I didn't know what Eleven was, but she blocked and dodged every blow that I aimed. She was everywhere and nowhere. She spun over my head, she ran up the mirror. While she whirled about my head, I felt that she was not really aiming her knife for me. Her spin moves were making me dizzy, and the reflections didn't help. At one point I aimed my sword towards her but hit the reflection. I stung again, hitting the mirror on the opposite side, and her reflection screamed. I hopped into the mirror, met the reflection face to face, flipped her to the floor, and pinned her.

"You win, you win," she said laughing. The real Eleven was in the mirror. Eleven pushed me off of her. I was exhausted. Unfazed, Eleven strolled out of the hallway with enviable grace and swung the heavy door open to the casino of old. The crowd was majestic and fanciful. Eleven lingered at the door beckoning me to follow. "Come on, Rayla," she said. "We sisters have some catching up to do," she said.

Was I mesmerized? Every step that Eleven took, I followed. We walked back into the casino, this Hall of Games, as if nothing had happened. Perhaps nothing did. I thought of Moulan and our nonfights in her treasured virtual home on Planet Hope. That place was no more, but what was this?

"They're all doubles," Eleven said, as we moved along the walls of the casino. Each wall was flanked with decadent tapestries. "A few are Mermaids. But we thought this was a fitting home for what you, in your world, view as disposable," she said. "They have purpose here. They have their own identities. They even have their own names. Some humans make their way inside, like Winn or Delta, as you call him. But we're very particular."

"You're not human," I said, as we glided past men and women sliding red and black chips.

"Human is a very limited way of describing me," she said. "I'm very one with my universe," she said. "My universe," she repeated. We walked side by side, and then she darted to the room's core. She waved me over and, despite myself, I followed. The entire place spun around us like we were the axis of this world. Perhaps we were.

"Moulan doesn't know about this place," Eleven shared.

"Are you sure about that?" I asked.

"She knows there's some activity, but she doesn't know about this. Like I said, I created it myself."

"And you're telling me this because?"

"Because, You and Moulan had great things to say about you; and as another powerful one in this multiverse, I thought you deserved to know," Eleven said.

"You think I'll protect you," I said. "It's just a matter of time before Moulan figures it out," I added.

"But you want the AI to live," she said. "And I want us to be friends," she added.

"Look, Planet Hope is on the other side of that door," Eleven said, pointing to the golden double doors at the end of the hall. "You ride the strings and it'll take you straight to Shogun City," she added.

"And what about the sea?" I asked.

Eleven giggled. "It's too late for that. We were in that hallway for over a month." Over a month? I thought of Carcine looking for me. I thought about the Winn/Delta. Was he distraught? What happened? "There's no returning to the sea, there's no Mermaid life. You're back to plain ole you again," she said, brushing her hair back with her palm. I glared at her.

"So you don't trust me," Eleven added. "I get it. No one does."

"What are you, Eleven?" I asked.

"That's not important," she quipped. "But on occasion, I grant wishes. You want to go home, take it while you can." I headed for the door, passing the dizzying crowd of gamers, all now oblivious to me. As I stood at the golden door, queasiness hit my stomach. This wasn't right. My eyes darted around the game room. No, this was not right. I ran through the crowd, opened the door to the hallway of mirrors, dipped through the reflection, and ran full force to the opposite door. It swung open to the universe, and I hopped out. I closed my eyes as I stepped into the blackness.

I waited for the fall. I waited to float. When I felt nothing, I opened my eyes and suddenly I was in the white topless car with Carcine. His foot mashed the breaks, and we flew through the streets. A bevy of dark cars were chasing us. Gunshots were fired. A few whizzed by my head. Carcine pushed my head down.

"Stay low," he shouted. We braked at the shore. He hopped out the car, I did the same.

"Hurry," he said. I kicked off my shoes. We both ran into the water; the sun was midway through the sea. We swam and swam. Bullets flew over our heads. The saltwater stung my eyes; and just as we swam far enough into the sea, I heard Winn Delta shout. I don't know where he was shouting from. Was he in the casino? Were the cries in my mind. I refused to turn around to see. "Nooooo," I heard him bellow. My legs were fins now, and I dipped below. Carcine was beside me.

Below the water we dipped through caverns. Carcine guided me through the dark seas. We swam through a dark, long cave; and when we exited through the opposite side, I was hit with the glow of the green Sphinx. But the glow's allure escaped me. I moved as quickly as possible through the underwater currents, Carcine still at my side. The temperature dropped. We were now in Martian waters.

"You're almost there," he said. "We'll meet again," he added and swam off. With the flip of a tail, Carcine was gone. Typical. I could see the cavern to the cove. I moved swiftly, pushing past exhaustion. My fins morphed to legs; my scuba gear had returned; and as I approached the rocky terrain in the cove, a hand dipped in to help me, but I climbed the rock and pushed myself up instead. Once above water, I removed my face guard. A wide-eyed Jason was kneeling beside me.

"Quite the trip," he said. His eyes sparkled with irony. I didn't speak, choosing to focus on my breath instead. I grabbed my belongings, strapped them on my back and climbed up the rock and out the glistening cavern. Jason followed. Above ground, we marched to our flying machine. I opened the door, Jason did the same. We both strapped in and flew off.

***

Back at Jason's place I was still speechless. I had no words for the experience. Notia was pelting me with questions, but she quickly realized that I was not in a speaking mood. She hugged me instead. But I was numb to her touch, numb to this world out of water. It was time to leave. "I'm ready," I said. Notia grabbed her things, Jason did the same. I held the vision of Planet Hope so clearly I nearly cried. We were there in an instant.

Chapter 18

Star Kitty

I stayed in bed for a week. I wasn't ill. I simply had no words for what had just transgressed, and the thought of attempting to explain it made me nauseous. Sui Lee brought me warm kale soup. Kent would sit at my side and read from The Book of Hope. He was affable around me, but I could feel his cloaked disgust. Delta visited with snarky updates about the planet councils. He didn't talk about his Merman transformation, and I was glad for it.

"Speak when you're ready," he said, taking my hand in his. "You know I understand." Day turned into night, and I was transfixed by the shifting shadows the dawning and setting light recarved like clockwork. The big red sun we danced around was nothing more than a universal timer, in this world at least. I'd danced around its rays enough to know that even this timer was relative. There are other suns.

Jason arrived on the seventh day, while Notia was in the room with me singing Erykah Badu hymns. When he arrived, Notia stood to leave and I spoke for the first time.

"Stay," I said. Notia shrugged her narrow shoulders and obliged. She nestled into a large white pillow on the floor. Jason was a bit sheepish. He pulled a handmade wooden chair near

Notia, took a seat, and smiled.

"I'm glad you're feeling better," he said.

"Where did you go?" I asked. I sat up in the bed, Notia rushed to my side to adjust my pillow, but I didn't need her help.

"I was going to ask you the same thing," he said. "I think we both had our own experience."

"Was it like being a firefly?" I asked him. Jason smiled warmly. His eyes were clear. His thoughts were concise. Before me sat a man who was not confused or bewildered by the turn of events.

"I was in the Hall of Games," he said, matter-of-factly.

"So was I," I added. "I didn't see you."

"And I didn't see you," he added."I guess we weren't playing the same game," he said. "I was in an ancient arcade—1980s Romania Earth, I believe," he said.

"I was in a casino," I added, "in the sands."

"I was in a city, a Romanian city, many decades ago. Did you see Eleven?" he asked.

I nodded. "She spoke of a city for doubles." I said. "I saw it."

"I saw her, too. She introduced me to other Originals in hiding—all gamers. The game of choice was Pac Man," he said. "And yours?"

"Poker," I said. "And what do they want?" I asked.

"That's the funny thing," he said. "They're perfectly happy where they are. They have no interest in returning. And what about your doubles?"

"They were happy to have a life," I shared, not that I asked them. I pushed off the covers and swung my legs over the bed. My feet dangled, and when they touched the floor they were flush with cold. Notia motioned to help me, but I waved her away and stood on my own. Slowly, I walked to the window. Our city skyline was a sight to behold, but I no longer found comfort in its steely beauty.

"I should leave," Notia said, looking from me to Jason. She slipped out of the room with a dancer's form, shutting the door behind her.

"It's a pretty city," Jason said, studying me carefully. "You've done wonders with it."

"You're not happy here anymore than I am," I said.
Jason, again, answered me with a steady smile before speaking.

"It's not that I don't like Planet Hope," he said. "I just wrestle with life in 3D. That's all. But the discoveries are compelling," he added, leaning back in his chair and raising an eyebrow. "Although, things would be much easier if I devoted my life to painting. Then I wouldn't have to wrestle with the words to explain it all." A faint rainbow morphed in the horizon. It stretched from the window to the balcony doors on the opposite side of the room.

"Painting a rainbow is much more thrilling than explaining light refractions," Jason said. "But Romania was nice."

The door to the balcony glistened with the setting sun. I inched towards the entrance, and Jason jumped up to escort me. On the balcony, I hoped that the soft breeze would be my anchor. Maybe the juxtaposition of coolness on my cheeks and ankles with the warmth of the emblazoned setting sun would trigger something. The gown I wore was thin and flitted with the breeze. I needed this moment. I needed this rainbow.

"You're like me," Jason said. "You're solo in your insights and a mystery for all those who question you. If you're looking for someone who understands, you've found him," he said. I could feel Jason's dark eyes narrowing in on me, but I chose to admire the miraculous light refractions. I liked Jason. He was overly practical but generous with his sensitivities. Although he spent ample time explaining his origins, he remained a mystery to most, as did I. There was something about the irony of a man whose honesty made him an enigma that was exciting to me. And he wasn't trying to be my protector. We weren't bonded by a complex past nor linked by a possible future. We were in the moment. "It is nice to know that they are happy. The Originals, I mean," said Jason, speaking of his encounter with the fireflies turned gamers in his Hall of Games. "I was relieved to know that I wasn't alone. But connecting with them felt like living in my past, an unfamiliar past. Perhaps it was someone else's past, and living up to that expectation of a time long gone didn't sit well with me. I don't want to go back. It was unsettling. Did your experience remind you of living in the past?" he asked.

"No," I said quietly. "It was like being in the present. But I was living a life that wasn't my own. I was trapped. I was uncomfortable in my own skin," I said. I'm uncomfortable in my own skin here, too; but I didn't share that fact with Jason, although he could sense it. I'm sure he sensed many things.

"Do you think you'll see the doubles again?" he asked.

"I hope not," I said.

"Is Eleven really your sister?" he asked.

"No," I retorted. Jason was sizing me up. I continued to take in the rainbow avoiding Jason's wanton stare.

"You don't know, do you? It's okay not to know...sometimes," he added. "For example, I have no idea why I'm standing here, but I like it." We laughed and I threw my arms around Jason to give him a swarthy hug. He hugged back slowly, almost as if he'd never been washed in affection before. Maybe he hadn't. He slowly wrapped his arms around me and squeezed back.

I thought of Delta. Our friendship was weighted with ironclad pasts and regulated futures. This moment with Jason was a floating cloud in the sky. I wanted to be in the cloud.

"I'm not very good with emotion," Jason said. "I feel but I can't articulate it."

"Join the club," I remarked, and we stood there on the balcony embraced under the arc of a brilliant light refraction.

"If I teach you how to play Pac Man will you teach me poker?" he asked.

"I'll think about it," I said, squeezing tighter. We stood there, holding one another until the sun set and our looming rainbow faded away.

Chapter 19

Make Me Over

I shared my story of the Hall of Games and the water journey before the eagerly awaiting council; and short of a few peppered gasps, they were rendered speechless. I stood in the rose-colored chambers I was once so familiar with, feeling like a near stranger in my own land. I was a walking mystery in their midst, a walking mystery amongst a bevy of myths. I counted the seconds of silence just to amuse myself.

"We need to alert the Shangos of Shogun City," Eartha said softly. She, too, was still taking in the gravity of the matter. She looked to the sky. "Perhaps there's a way that they can...."

"Block the waters," Kent continued, interrupting Eartha curtly. "That's like putting a blanket over the sky. It's impossible, he said, exasperated.

"I thought you were a man of possibility, Kent," Diva chimed. She adjusted in her seat and arched her back, stretching for a potential spar with words. Diva was anxious. The others were silenced in their confusion. But Kent's simmering anger was slowly boiling over. Lagos placed his large hands over a bowl of crystals, enhancing their frequency to balance everyone's off kilter mood.

"I said to stay away from the waters," Kent affirmed "No one ever listens to me."

"At least now we know," said Eartha, with the firm matronly warmth we'd come to know her for. "The doubles, AI have their own life. And Jason's fellow Original Originals are playing some video game in a time warp. Maybe dismantling the doubles under the guise of the Shangos wasn't the best idea. Now we know."

"Wonderful," Kent continued. "I'm glad you find some comfort in this, because I don't."

"I agree with Kent," Lagos added, his deep booming voice filling the room. Even seated, Lagos stood a head above everyone. "Moulan could very well be orchestrating a takeover with the Mermaids and the Original Originals, all under the guise of this Eleven," he said.

"And it sounds like Carcine is working with her," said Diva, cutting her eyes.

"Carcine is not working with anyone," I added calmly.

"You're not exactly partial," Diva snapped, tossing her head to the side. Diva always distrusted my loyalties to Planet Hope. I was a reminder of the time she'd lost, the daughter who'd vanished, and the messiness their lives had become. "Why are we believing her, anyway?" she asked.

"Are you referring to Eleven?" Eartha asked.

"I'm referring to her," said Diva, flipping her hand in my direction.

"Rayla's not a good determinant of character," Diva said. Her words were knives and she dug deeper. "How do we even know your story is true? It's absurd," she said. "And I, for one, am done with idolizing this child like she's got the answers of a second coming. She knows nothing. She's absent from council meetings. She gives us these ridiculous stories about Mermen and games in sands, and we suck it all up like it's manna from the sky. She is nothing but a prop by Moulan."

"Wait a minute," Kent interrupted.

"No, you wait a minute, Kent," Diva said standing. She was petite but her presence was tall and the council floated on her airy cries. "She is nothing but a mouthpiece for that heretic, Moulan, whom we followed off the cliff that got us into this mess in the first place; and I refuse to stand by idly, while everyone showers her with empathy. Empathy for what? She goes underwater, bumps her head, and hallucinates. She dreams up colorful stories with her good-for-nothing boyfriend Carcine, who couldn't even save our planet and disappeared into the throngs of nothingness. She watches Moulan transform Delta, our President's son, into a Merman, and we're all supposed to be in awe? Have you all gone mad! Am I the only one who remembers what happened to us? Moulan tricked us, hijacked time and space, sent us into the abyss, lost in time on purpose. I don't trust any space she's in, and I don't trust this daughter of hers. Our reality is Moulan's fiction. Who is to say this is even Rayla standing before us? She's nothing but a Moulan clone."

A clone? I am not a clone. I looked to Kent, but his eyes were beaming lasers honed in on Diva.

"That's enough," Kent said, at a pitch so low I thought the temperature would drop.

"Oh, say it isn't so, Kent. Can you honestly say you fathered this girl? She's an experiment—a test. We were there," Diva screamed.

"That's enough," Kent repeated, hammering the words, but it was too late. I felt the heat rising from my chest to my temple. The room was still, but my mind was spinning, and the eyes of the council's former Neo Astronauts were white hot on my skull. Kent stood and called my name, but his voice faded. I only heard the white noise in my head.

A clone. An experiment. A smile stretched across my face so

wide I thought my cheeks would snap. Wouldn't that just explain everything, I thought, laughing to myself. My mouth smiled. My eyes did not. I saw Eartha standing, leaning over the council table as she banged her fist, yelled at Diva, but her words were muted in my mind.

A clone. An experiment. I'd laugh aloud if it didn't feel so true. Fortunately, Sui Lee wasn't in the room to hear this melee. But her calming presence would have prevented this outburst from arising. Maybe it was fate that she had another matter to attend to. I heard someone whimpering about an apology. but my anger had taken the swoop of a silent storm.

"There's no need for an apology," I said. My voice was clear and sane. Again, all eyes were on me.

"I'm just telling the truth," Diva yelled, pleading for pity. Her mouth was exaggerating the syllables as if she were speaking in slow motion. "What kind of world are we building if we can't tell the truth?"

"You can't tell my truth," I heard myself say.

"I said that's enough," Kent shouted, his voice reverberated like a terra quake. The rumble felt good, too good, and then it broke. I don't even know what "it" was; but this it, something deep within me ruptured. I was free. Free from what? I didn't know, but suddenly I was not the woman I was a few moments ago. I was a new Rayla. I was in my own skin.

"Rayla," Eartha shouted. Lagos felt the rupture, too, and ran toward me. He leaped over the table, hoping to stop my flow. And before the others could look my way, I was already in motion. I envisioned the Field of the Yellow Lady and the empty space where Moulan's cottage once glistened. I held the vision dear, I saw it clearly and in a sliced second I was there. Delta, much like Lagos a moment earlier, was running full speed through the field toward me. But he wouldn't make it. "Rayla," he called. I wasn't listening.

Where Moulan's cottage once stood, a small ivy-laced lagoon

had emerged. Was it a result of the geyser Jason sparked? Regardless, it was my homecoming. I dived in. My legs became fins and a path of neon green light shined before me, lighting a brilliant trail that I eagerly followed. I knew the way, and my newfound radiance deepened with each flow. I felt the hollow worry of worlds and words fall away. And as I neared the glowing Sphinx, the dark-haired Mermaid with her classic black tail flitted by the entrance.

"Sister," Eleven cooed.

She was not my sister, but I was happy to see her. I swam through the golden gates, and the sea of striking Mermen and Mermaids circled in seamless formation. Eleven swam beside me and guided me to a purple dwelling of crystals.

"For you," she said, "your home." Much like Moulan's underwater dwelling, this place too was waterless. When we entered its energy field, our fins morphed back to legs and we strolled inside.

"I'd like to be alone," I told her. "Don't get used to it," she said, and moved on.

What was I doing? I didn't know but I liked it.

Chapter 20

Formation

SOMETHING had come over me. I'd raced through time and back; but not since those early years on Planet Hope when Sui Lee held me in my arms had I ever felt home. This water world and its protected spaces was the home I sought. Planet Hope in all its efforts to begin anew didn't feel like this; and I didn't know what I could do, if anything, to get it there.

And for the moment, I no longer cared. I fell into the lush sofa in my new dwelling, threw my head back, and sighed. I closed my eyes and let the blackness of my inner space blanket me.

"So you like it here?" Eleven asked with a keen pointedness. I opened my eyes reluctantly to answer her. I wanted her to leave. Why couldn't I just sleep?

"I just think, if we're sisters, we should get to know one another," she said, now seated on a black chair across from me. But there was no urgency in answering Eleven either. I closed my eyes, but the rustle and clacking of beads reawakened me. Someone had entered. I opened my eyes once again, and You in a sleek turquoise gown was taking a seat in a golden chair across the room. The three of us formed a pyramid.

"We've been thinking," You began. Her eyes were beguiling while Eleven's were needles. Both were images of me. Both weren't me. You was AI of sorts and Eleven was, well, I didn't know what she was. While their presence in the Hall of Games was terror-filled, here in his space I called home they were mere shadows of their scarier selves.

"We've been thinking," You continued. "That we should merge."

"Merge?" I asked. My voice was heavy but the weight of the world was slipping away.

"Yes. Merge," Eleven continued. "We think that if we all functioned as one, then…"

"Then these worlds would be a better place," You continued.

"In these spaces," Eleven added. "We feel limited."

"Yes, limited," You echoed.

"But if we merged…,." she continued.

My drowsiness had no bearing on my clarity. Why wouldn't these women let me sleep? Was a goodnight's sleep just impossible in this universe?

"Merged? How are we supposed to do that?" I asked. "Are we merging powers? merging worlds?" Eleven rose and slid toward me. She took a seat at one side. You stood and took a seat at the other.

"We're all part of you," Eleven continued. "We don't know how we were fragmented, but we figure that if we merge….."

"Merge?" I repeated.

"See, I'm not really artificial intelligence," You said, taking my hand in hers.

I was recreated using your DNA, but I can only do so much."

"As for me," Eleven added, "well, we're sisters. And if we merged...," her voice trailed off like a far-off lullaby.

"How are we sisters?" I asked. My eyelids were heavy, but I forced them open. Listening to both of them was like hearing my own echo.

"Because Moulan said so," she continued. Her voice softened as did the light in the room.

"We're fragmented souls," You continued."And we figured, that with you, we'd be whole."

"You're a fragmented soul," Eleven added, nestling her head in my neck. "Don't we make you feel whole?"

"And complete?" You chimed sweetly.

"If we merged we could be superhuman," Eleven cooed.

"Indomitable," You added. "One. Don't you want to be one?"

"Whole," Eleven bellowed.

"Aren't you happy here?" they said in harmony. Their voices rose and fell like melodies in a song, and finally I was lulled back to a state of near sleep. I relaxed.

"Yes," I said, before I could give their hefty chatter any thought. "Yes, I am." For the first time in a long time or maybe it was for the first time ever, I felt at peace. Then I fell asleep.

Chapter 21

Amoeba Cleansing Syndrome

I awakened on the floor. I thought of the hall in the Crystal Cove, but this was no Crystal Cove. I was in my home. My water space home. I recognized a few collectibles from my protected room in Shogun City. You must have done the decorating, no doubt. An elegant red-feathered fan was posted on the wall, a reminder of Rayla Redfeather. I had a record player with a Stevie Wonder album, and a bowl of turquoise crystals sat in a glass bowl placed on an old oak table. Midnight-blue beads hung from the ceiling, separating one room from the next. How many rooms were in this home? A porcelain teapot with blue flowers sat on a silver plate. Someone had made a fresh pot of tea. I poured the dark liquid into the matching palm-sized cups and drank when I heard the beaded clacking ring again. Moulan, decked in her green gown regalia and lime sea shell ornaments sauntered in from the back room.

Something had changed within me. Moulan was neither friend nor foe. As for the blood that bound us, in this water space world, it no longer felt relevant. She stood in her magical ware more reminiscent of a dream I'd had than of a woman I knew. The reality was I didn't know Moulan. I didn't know the new Planet Hope. For the first time, I felt that there was no consequence to any of it. Ignorance, for the moment, was bliss.

“You want some?” I asked, holding up the teapot.

“I’m the one who serves tea around here,” she quipped, as if the formality was hers and hers alone.

“Yeah well, welcome to my world,” I said cavalierly. I poured another cup and doused it back. What was I saying? “You might wanna’ knock next time. I’m not up for drop-in visitations. Can you knock in underwater vortexes?”

Moulan looked at me as if I was unrecognizable. I flipped open a little green box of tiny brown cakes and ate one. Wonder who brought these in?

“They’re good,” I said, my mouth still full of sweetness. I caught a few crumbs as they fell from my mouth.

“You’re different,” Moulan said quietly. The sincerity in her voice would have frightened me, that is, if I’d cared.

“Whatever,” I said with a sniff. I poured another cup of tea and carried it with me to the opposite side of the room. My mild sarcasm was neither a deflector nor defense. ‘You’re different,’ I repeated in my head. I was born different and I was indifferent to the nonmatters at hand. Someone had assembled a small bookshelf. Rather than stand idly under Moulan’s puzzled gaze, I moved over to the bookshelf and studied the bindings. No title caught my eye; and Moulan, in her annoyance, marched over and stood in front of me.

“I was really hoping for some alone time,” I told her. “I was hoping we girlies could bond,” she said, forcing a half smile.

“You can’t be serious,” I chuckled. “You didn’t learn enough about me when you fought me before?”

I moved on, fell into the coral green couch made of moss and seaweed. Moulan plopped down beside me.

"I just think that we have a lot to talk about, and we could catch up and...," her voiced thinned. "Don't you have some emotions you want to work out?"

"Moulan," I said. "I really don't care. I don't care who you are, why you're here, what this world is about. I don't care what happened between you and my father. I simply don't care. The time to answer these questions was many rotations ago and in my, shall we say, evolution, I simply don't care."

"I don't believe that," she said with a sniffle.

"Believe what you want," I said. "I'm chill."

"Where did you learn that word?" she snapped.

"Who cares," I said.

"You're just adjusting to underwater life. We all start off with a sense of nonchalance and relative indifference. It's a freeing at first. But that too shall pass."

I stretched my arms out across the back of the couch and crossed my legs. Short of Moulan's looming presence, I liked this protected space. Moulan's chatter was nothing more than modest whimpers. I was more transfixed by the ebullience of the silence in between.

"Have you seen You and Eleven," she said sheepishly, her green eyes softening. What was with these questions? My annoyance grew.

"You're looking at them," I snapped.

"You merged?" she said, as she sat erect and inched away. "And you weren't going to tell me about it?"

"It's a joke," I said. "We didn't merge," I added. "They're out swimming about or whatever it is they do down here."

"But are you considering it?" she asked, sitting up and scooting to the edge of the couch. I stood and poured another cup of tea. She obviously wasn't going anywhere.

"What difference does it make?" I thought about my question and rephrased it. "What difference does it make to you?"
"Well, I kind of like the way you are as is," she said, watching me closely. "I like your innocence, your bedazzled curiosity. Your vulnerability. Vulnerability is important." I ignored her. I had just awakened and already I was looking forward to the lull of sleep. "I like the other girls, too. I just think you work very nicely apart."

"As fragmented parts of a whole?" I snapped.

"It's more interesting than being a firefly," she quipped, wrinkling her nose.

"Am I really an experiment?" I asked her. Moulan floated over to the teapot and poured a glass. She tossed it back, and floated in a circle.
"We're all experiments," she said. "Haven't you figured that out yet?"

"I don't believe that I am," I said.

"I'm sure that's a belief that serves you," she said. She floated about the room, studying the assortment of hybrid adornments. Finally, she whipped around, planted one hand on one hip while sticking out the other.

"Oh, for octopus sake, do you want to create your own universe or not?" she asked.

"Why would I want to do that?" I asked.

"Why?Why?Why?," she said. "Why this and why that? Why is why the question?" she asked, throwing her hands in the air like she was tossing bushels of flowers to an audience of spectators. "Why would anyone want power? Why would anyone want to create their own life? Why would anyone want to have their own rules. Why? Why?

Why?" Moulan fell to her knees.

"Why?" she asked, her voice shooting up an octave."Why not?" she said, her voice dropped into the depths of her stomach, her head and arms dropped to the floor, too. I just looked at her as she crouched in a ball on the floor.

Seconds later she shot up, her knees still planted in the floor."Why?" she screamed, stretching her arms out and arching her back. She hung her head back as if waiting for lightening to strike. When the imaginative storm passed, she composed herself, grabbed her skirt with her thumb and index finger, stood erect, and glared. "Read my book," she commanded. She snatched a green-laced book off the tiny bookshelf and hurled it at me. I ducked, the book hit the tapestry covered wall behind me, and fell in my lap.

"This one I wrote myself," she quipped. "If you have any questions, I'll be in another universe drinking from a pineapple." With that, Moulan spun, her skirt wrapping around her. She spun and spun until her green gorgeous gown was all a blur. She kept spinning and then she was gone. I looked to the book on my lap. The book was already open. An image of a giant green pineapple was etched on the page. I pulled my red feather from my hair, slipped it in the binding, and shut the book. On the back was a sketch of a spinning Moulan. I flipped the book to the front and saw glowing green eyes staring back at me.

"This isn't the same book you gave me before," I said aloud. In a flash, Moulan reappeared, in a green-feather headdress twice her size and short mint-green dress speckled with jade jewels and blades of bluegrass. She wore sparkles on her ankles. She didn't have on any shoes, and she clutched a giant green pineapple in her hands.

"My story changes, pineapple thief. If you're lucky, yours will, too," Moulan snapped. She flashed a grin, wiggled her hips, and stomped one foot on the ground three times. Then she vanished again. I waited, wondering if she'd reappear for the fun of it. She didn't, of course. My own universe? I shook my head. Perhaps now I could get some sleep.

***

I wouldn't be down here long—maybe just long enough to read this Moulan epic and relax. We may all be experiments; but there were other dimensions to this space, other hands at play, and I felt a responsibility to uncover them. I felt responsible for uncovering all of me while being squarely more of me in the quest. That's not asking too much. No, that's not asking too much at all.

Chapter 22

Le Chevelier de Saint-Georges

"I Want to Leave This Planet" - Charles Earland

WINN Kincot sat at the edge of the Mediterranean awaiting his queen. He'd assembled the shells and oregano as always, lighting the candle just as the New Moon rose. She would appear, eventually. And deep in the horizon he saw her. Numidya rose from the depths of the sea, floating on the water's surface towards him. Her hair was black. Her tail transformed, and within seconds she was walking ashore without a trace of water on her skin.

"I missed you," Winn said, taking Numidya's arm in his as they walked ashore.

"Do you need rest?" he asked.

"I'm here to play," she said slyly. "You know where to take me."

"Will we be using the same cues?" he asked.

"Just wait for me to say the word eleven then you'll know what to do," she said. The twosome marched off the sands. A white topless car was parked in the distance. Lights off, Carcine watched the duo trek through the sands to the street. Yes, this was Numidya alright. But it wasn't Rayla. A part of him was glad it wasn't. He watched Winn walk Numidya to a dark car, and the two pulled off. Too bad he missed the return cycle a few months ago. His Merman life, it seemed, was over. Things could be worse, he thought. At least he wasn't on Planet Hope.

***

Delta stood at the edge of the Field of the Yellow Lady. No, this ivy-spruced lagoon where Moulan's home once stood was a new development. He took a seat at the field's edge, not wanting to get too close to the waters but not wanting to leave it either. Rayla, he figured, would emerge from it soon. He'd been out here some weeks now, but he liked camping out in the open air. It reminded him of the days with his troops of old. Delta saw the bubbles first. There was no reason for a lagoon of this nature to bubble over. First he saw a flight of brightly lit fireflies hovering. But when a figure emerged, he froze. A woman with dark hair pulled back in a ponytail climbed out of the sea like she'd lived there her whole life. No Mermaid's tale, she rose from the water like a flower from soil. Her clothing was all black, skin-like and shiny. She looked about like it was her first time on land, stretching her arms to the sky and breathing in air as if for the first time. It didn't take long for her to feel Delta's presence. It's not like he'd camouflaged himself. Delta stood and nodded his head. He remained frozen as this woman slid toward him.

"Do you know who I am?" she asked.

"You're Eleven. Eleven Brown," Delta said.

"And you didn't want to come to the sea to find me, so I came to you," she said.

"I see," he continued.

"Are you going to show me around, or am I going to have to fig ure out this terra myself," she asked, rotating her shoulders and twisting her neck in a continuous stretch.

"Where's Rayla?" he asked.

"Doing what Rayla always does," said Eleven. "Figuring out the mysteries of the world, reading Moulan's saga. Who knows how long that will take." Delta was still in trance. He shook it off.

"You know, I'll have to take you before the council," he said.

"So soon? I was hoping I could play around a bit first. You don't honestly think I'm going to let you escort me to the council. Why would I do that?"

"Why would you come back at all?" Delta asked. "I thought you were gone for good."

"I did go for good. And now I'm back. Where's Jason?" she asked.

"Back at home, I assume," he said. Eleven pecked him on the cheek. Then she kissed Delta on his lips. He didn't resist. Eleven marched on. She knew this Field of the Yellow Lady like she knew the back of her hand. She just never thought in a thousand years that she'd come back. Hopefully, Rayla will merge, she thought. That would be so much fun.

***

In a small town in Romania, a wise man with a knack for wanderers managed to get his hands on a few of the latest games sweeping the west. He watched the young man with the dark hair and red T-shirt playing Pac Man with the vivaciousness of a football player. This Jason kid loved games. He stayed in the arcade with the others 'til closing. On some nights, the shopkeeper kept it open just so the kid wouldn't have to go home. One day, in a flit of charity, the shopkeeper told the kid he could take the game home. "If you can wheel it out of here it's yours."

The young man was delighted.

***

The council didn't give Jason the biggest crystal dome on the planet. In fact, the one they gifted him was rather modest. But he didn't care. As long as he had his painting and his Pac Man game, he was content. He'd even managed to get a galactic game going simultaneously with some of the people in Romania, although he wasn't sure whom he was playing against. Whoever it was, was dead set on winning. He hoped his overall top score would be higher than theirs.

Rayla should have learned this game, he thought. He hoped she would return soon. If he could maintain the top score, he could ensure that she would return safely. That's all he could do on this side at least; that is, unless he unleashed the fireflies. And why would he want to do that? 'Yes, Rayla, please hurry,' he thought. He desperately wanted to paint her in red feathers with a backdrop of shining fireflies. Or better yet, he could paint her as head of the not-so-fabled Mermaid Marines. But until then, he'd keep the top score. There's nothing like winning the long game.

Biography

Ytasha L. Womack is an award winning author and filmmaker. She's an international ambassador for Afrofuturism and the imagination. Her works include *Afrofuturism: The World of Black Sci Fi and Fantasy Culture*, *Rayla 2212*, *Post Black*, and *Beats Rhymes and Life: What We Love and Hate About Hip Hop*. Her book *Afrofuturism* is a Locus Awards Finalist and a leading primer on the subject. She's director of the highly anticipated sci fi film *Bar Star City*. A Chicago native, she can be found dancing to house music and drinking unusual amounts of tea.

CPSIA information can be obtained at www.ICGtesting.com
Printed in the USA
LVOW07s1841201016

509597LV00011B/741/P